THE HEREFORDSHIRE HANGMEN

A captivating Victorian historical murder mystery

KERRY TOMBS

Inspector Ravenscroft Detective Mysteries Book 8

JOFFE BOOKS

Revised edition 2020
Joffe Books, London
www.joffebooks.com

First published in Great Britain 2017

**Join our mailing list and become one of 1,000s of
readers enjoying free Kindle crime thriller, detective,
mystery, and romance books and new releases.
Receive your first bargain book this month!**

www.joffebooks.com

We love to hear from our readers! Please email any
feedback you have to: feedback@joffebooks.com

ISBN 978-1-78931-558-5

PROLOGUE

MALVERN HILLS, OCTOBER 1891

'Sorry to have called you out here at such a late hour, sir, but it is not every day that we find a body hanging from a tree.'

'No, I suppose not, Sergeant,' said Ravenscroft. He held his lantern aloft to light the way over the uneven ground for himself and Constable Crabb. 'Who discovered the body?'

'Some old farm labourer out walking his dog.'

'I wonder what he was doing up here on such an inclement evening,' remarked Constable Crabb from behind them.

Ravenscroft paused to recover his breathing, and to wipe the driving rain away from his spectacles.

'I should warn you both, it is not a pleasant sight.'

'I understand. Death seldom is.' They drew near to the swaying corpse. 'Good grief!' exclaimed Ravenscroft.

'Some of the birds have had a go at him, but thought it better if we left him where he was until you had seen him.'

'That is quite right, Sergeant. The poor fellow.' Ravenscroft brought the lantern closer to inspect the body. 'Evidently someone tied one end of the rope round that branch, and the other round his neck, before pulling the victim off the ground.'

'Shall we take him down, sir?'

'Yes, Sergeant. I suppose that would be the kindest thing to do.'

The sergeant addressed two uniformed officers who stood nearby. 'Here, you men take hold of his legs while I climb up this tree.'

Ravenscroft turned away from the body.

'Why go to all this trouble? Who the devil would want to hang a man out here in this godforsaken place?' asked a visibly shaken Crabb.

'Who indeed?' Ravenscroft turned up his collar against the cold wind and driving rain that was blowing across the hill.

'Easy there, men, get ready to catch hold of him as I cut the rope,' said the sergeant, edging slowly along the branch.

'Who found this man?' asked Ravenscroft.

'I did, sir.' An elderly man with a ruddy complexion and untidy hair emerged from the darkness.

'And you are?'

'Caleb Robinson, your honour,' replied the man, removing his cap.

'When did you find the body?'

'Just after six o'clock tonight, your worship.'

'I am not "your honour," nor "your worship." And what were you doing up here on top of this hill, at that hour? It must have been getting quite dark by then?'

'I was taking Jasper here out for his evening walk.'

Ravenscroft looked down at the old sheepdog standing by Caleb Robinson's side. The animal let out a bark of acknowledgement.

'Not the most suitable place for a walk?' suggested Constable Crabb.

'Well, we comes up here most evenings. Jasper, he just loves to run over the hills,' grinned the old man, exposing a jagged set of uneven, stained teeth. 'It were Jasper here who found him.'

'Did you come up here yesterday?' asked Ravenscroft.

'Yes, sir.'

2

'And I presume that the man was not here then?'

'Course not. I would have reported it then, wouldn't I?' retorted Robinson, his companion growling at the detective.

Ravenscroft smiled briefly. 'Quite. And where do you live, Mr Robinson?'

'Over at Eastnor, in the cottage next to the Post Office.'

'I know it well,' said Crabb.

'Rather a long way to come for an evening walk on such an inclement night,' suggested Ravenscroft.

'Not really. There's a short cut through Deer Park, and up through the woods — and it weren't raining when we left home.'

'He was dead when you found him?'

'I suppose he were. I didn't stop to take a closer look at him, but he weren't twitching, or moaning, or anything like that,' replied Robinson with some degree of relish.

'So what did you do then?'

'I walked all the way down the path to the inn below on the road. They sent a lad on a horse to the police station in Ledbury. We waited at the inn until your sergeant arrived.'

'You did well, Mr Robinson.'

'Easy there, lads! Lower him to the ground,' instructed the sergeant before clambering down from the tree.

'Tell me, Mr Robinson, when you and your dog were making your way across the hills this evening, did you happen to pass by anyone else?'

'No, I don't think so.' He scratched his head. 'But then again maybe I did? Or maybe I didn't? No, I don't recall seeing anyone.'

'Well did you or did you not pass anyone on the way up here?' persisted Ravenscroft, annoyed at the witness's shifting uncertainty.

'No. There was only that horse.'

'What horse?'

'I heard a horse's bridle jingling in the wood.'

'Did you see who was riding this horse?' asked Ravenscroft eagerly.

'No. I said I only heard the sound of a horse. I never said I saw it,' said Robinson irritably.

'I see. Constable Crabb, let us see what we can find out about this poor fellow,' said Ravenscroft, turning away from the man and his dog, and bringing the lantern closer to the body on the ground. 'Male; age probably late twenties in years; unshaven; ruddy brown complexion suggesting that he worked out of doors; generally unkempt appearance; a labourer of some kind by the state of his worn clothes. There is a small scar on his left cheek. There appear to be no obvious signs of death other than by strangulation. I would think he has been here for some hours. Let me look at his hands. Some wear, but not excessively so, suggesting that although our victim was from the poorer classes he was not engaged in heavy manual labour; no ink stains on the fingers, so obviously he was not a clerk. Has anyone here seen this man before?'

'No, sir,' replied the sergeant and the two constables, almost in unison.

'Mr Robinson?'

'Stranger to me, your honour.' Jasper gave another bark. 'Get back there, boy.'

'Let us examine his pockets to see if there are any clues to his identity,' said Ravenscroft, passing over the lantern to Crabb.

The group stood in silence watching the detective as he conducted his search.

'Completely empty — no money, no papers, not even a pocket watch. There is a hole, however, in his coat pocket. I wonder if anything might have slipped through the lining? Ah, what is this?' said Ravenscroft, standing upright.

The small audience edged forwards.

'A small round pill box. It says "Doctor Gazzey's Wonder Pills" on the lid. That is interesting. Still three left inside. What condition was he taking these for? I suspect it is probably some kind of quack medicine. Anyway, I suggest we get out of this unpleasant weather as soon as possible. Sergeant, would you and your men load the body on to the wagon, and then take

4

him to the hospital mortuary? We will see if a closer examination there will provide us with any additional information.'

'Yes, sir. Right, you men take hold of his legs. Let's be quick about it. We should have all been in our beds hours ago.'

'Thank you, Mr Robinson. You may go now. You did the right thing in informing us. We know where you are should we need to have further words with you.'

'Glad to have been of assistance.' Robinson raised his cap once more before he and his barking dog took their leave.

'Well, Tom, what brought our man up here on such a wet windy day as this?' asked Ravenscroft, as the two detectives watched the wagon and its load begin its slow journey down the hill.

'Perhaps he was killed elsewhere?' suggested Crabb.

'If that was so, why bring the body all the way up here, when it would have been easier to have left it in some ditch by the roadside? No, I think he had arranged to meet someone in this forlorn place, and that person, or persons, then killed him.'

'You think there could have been more than one of them?'

'Probably. One might have held the fellow upright, while the other pulled on the rope, although there is the possibility, I suppose, that one man could have rendered the victim senseless, before placing the knot round his neck and hauling him off his feet.'

'But if they killed him first, why go to the bother of hanging him from that tree, when they could have just left the corpse on the ground?' suggested Crabb.

'Yes, that is perplexing. Which brings us back to the more obvious conclusion: the victim was still alive when the rope was placed around his neck. Of course, a single man might have done it, using a horse as the gallows trapdoor — that is how they did it in the old days.'

'It is a dramatic way to kill a man. Whoever killed him must have gained some kind of satisfaction from watching the poor man die.'

'That could have been so, in which case the victim suffered a particularly unpleasant death. It may not even have been particularly quick, and there would have been no one else out here to have come to his assistance. It does not bear thinking about. A cold shiver ran down Ravenscroft's spine.

'What a way to go,' muttered an ashen-faced Crabb. 'No one deserves to die like that.'

'That man Robinson said he thought he heard the sound of a horse in the wood. I wonder if it had a rider — and if so, if its rider was our killer.'

'It could have been, sir.'

'Shame that Robinson did not see the horse. It is no good us returning tomorrow to see if we can discover some tracks in the wood. This heavy rain will have washed any remaining evidence away. Our man was murdered in a brutal fashion. Whoever killed him must have been acting out some kind of personal revenge, taking the law into his own hands. He, or they, obviously came fully prepared, hence the rope. We must find out, Tom, who has committed this terrible crime, but first we have to identify our victim. We will have a photograph taken of the poor man in the morning, and also circulate his description, as well as seeing if anyone locally has been reported as missing. This man may well have had a wife and children. He certainly had a father and mother. Someone will be missing him, and may wish to claim the body.'

'Yes, sir,' replied Crabb.

'Well there is nothing more we do out here tonight. Let us get out of this rain and wind, and return home. We have had more than our fair share of investigating crimes in these hills over the years. Good God, Crabb I have just realised something!' exclaimed Ravenscroft suddenly.

'What is it, sir?'

'I have just remembered the name of this hill. If my memory serves me correctly, we are standing right here — on Hangman Hill!'

CHAPTER ONE

LEDBURY

'Do you know, this fellow is really quite clever,' remarked Ravenscroft to his wife.

'Who is?' asked Lucy.

'Conan Doyle.'

The couple were sitting before an open fire in their cottage in Church Lane.

'Oh, you have been reading those stories again.'

'And very ingenious they are, as well. I have just completed "The Red-Headed League."' Ravenscroft removed his spectacles and wiped them vigorously on his handkerchief.

'What an unusual title,' remarked Lucy, looking up from her needlework.

'It's all about a pawnbroker who has red hair, and who answers an advertisement for red-headed men to undertake employment with an organisation entitled "The Red-Headed League." When he attends the interview he is successful in gaining the position, and every day afterwards he sits in the offices of the society, copying out pages from the *Encyclopaedia Britannica*, between the hours of ten in the morning and two in the afternoon.'

'What a strange thing to do.'

'Well, Sherlock Holmes takes up the case, and discovers that the only reason why the red-headed pawnbroker was paid to copy out these pages, is so that a group of unsavoury characters can gain access to his shop premises during his absence, when they can go down into his cellar and start digging a tunnel.' Ravenscroft replaced his spectacles and leaned forwards as he warmed to his narrative.

'And why were these men digging a tunnel under the pawnbroker's shop?' asked an intrigued Lucy.

'So that they could secure a way into the vaults of the nearby bank. In order to do so they had to make sure that the pawnbroker was out of the way, so that they could conduct their work without being detected. Brilliant idea, is it not?'

'I suppose your Sherlock Holmes solves the crime and apprehends the perpetrators?' asked Lucy.

'Of course; one would expect nothing less. Mr Doyle certainly has some imaginative ideas for his stories, although he based his detective Sherlock Holmes on a certain Auguste Dupin.'

'And who was this Auguste Dupin?'

'He was the creation of the American writer, Edgar Allan Poe. In his story "The Murders in the Rue Morgue," Dupin solves the mystery by deciphering certain clues that the murderer had left behind him at the scene of the crime. It was written about fifty years ago, I believe.'

'Was your Mr Doyle a policeman, before he took up writing?'

'A medical practitioner, I believe, but apparently writing detective stories pays more than attending to the sick.'

'Perhaps you should take up writing, Samuel. I am sure the public would like to know how you solved some of your greatest cases,' said Lucy, reaching for her needlework.

'I could not do that.'

'And why ever not? You could write all about those murders you have solved since you came to Ledbury, to say nothing about your earlier experiences in Whitechapel. I am sure that if you had still been there at the time of those terrible murders you would have caught that horrible Jack the Ripper in no time.'

'Maybe, but I was otherwise engaged in solving that crime in Worcester, and paying court to you, my dear. A far more important occupation,' smiled Ravenscroft. 'No, I don't think I would have the ability to put pen to paper. I don't have the patience, or the time.'

'You don't know what you could do until you try. As for the time, you are always complaining that you are bored because nothing happens in Ledbury for weeks on end.'

'Perhaps when I retire?'

'I am sure people will be most intrigued to learn how you arrived at your clever deductions. Look at the many criminals you have put behind bars.'

'I suppose there must have been quite a few. The problem is that a number of people who were involved in the cases might not like what I decide to write. It would all then become a question of confidentiality.'

'You could always change the names of the people, and even some of the details. One day the exploits of Samuel Ravenscroft may even come to rival those of the great Sherlock Holmes.'

'You are forgetting that Sherlock Holmes is not a real person, whereas I am.'

'Now you are just making excuses.'

'We will see,' Ravenscroft retreated behind his magazine, feeling that he was being backed into a corner.

'Have you had any further news about that poor man murdered on Hangman Hill?' asked Lucy, changing the subject.

'I am afraid not. It is now nearly three weeks since we found his body, and despite our issuing a description of the man to all the local newspapers, no one has yet come forward to identify him.'

'Perhaps he was a stranger to these parts?'

'You may be correct. It is most frustrating. All he had on him was that small box of pills. They were evidently some kind of quack medicine, for there are no details of "Doctor Gazzey's Pills" mentioned in any of the medical books. No, unless something happens quite soon, I fear we will be forced to abandon the case, although I would be loath to do that. I would still like to feel that we could secure some kind of justice for the poor man, by bringing his murderers to account.'

'What a terrible crime. I cannot imagine the agony he must have gone through. I am sure that something will happen quite soon.'

'I wish I shared your optimism. Let me see, what time is it?' asked Ravenscroft taking out his pocket watch. 'Twenty minutes past eight. I said I would meet Tom at the Mop Fair at around this time. We are not expecting any trouble; people are generally good-natured at these events, but you never know. I hope you will excuse me. I should not be gone for too long.'

'Samuel, I wonder if I might accompany you? I should so like to see the fair,' asked Lucy laying down her sewing.

'Of course, my dear. I will be glad of the company.'

* * *

'Good evening, Mrs Ravenscroft,' said the fresh-faced constable.

'Good evening to you, Tom,' replied Lucy. 'I have not seen you recently. I trust Jennie and the children are well?'

'Very well, Mrs Ravenscroft, although the young one does keep us awake at night.'

'I know,' smiled Lucy.

'And how are things, Tom?' asked Ravenscroft looking across the marketplace towards the streets full of crowded people.

'No problems, sir. Everyone seems quite happy. Some of the Leewood lads are in a boisterous mood, but I've had a word with them, and I've got the men at the ready should any trouble break out.'

'Then let us hope that they will not be needed. There are certainly a great many people here tonight. Shall we go and see what entertainment is on offer?' asked Ravenscroft, linking his wife's arm. 'I will see you later, Tom.'

The detective and Lucy made their way through the noisy crowds of people that flocked along the Homend, pausing now and then to look at the varied entertainment that was on offer from the numerous stalls and booths. A juggler was receiving applause as a group of musicians wandered up and down the street, and a number of children called out excitedly from a revolving carousel.

'Pretty ribbons for the lady,' said an old woman presenting her wares for Lucy to inspect.

'How much is the red one?' asked Lucy.

'Twopence, my lovely,' replied the woman.

'Could I have it, Samuel? It would go so well with my bonnet.'

'Of course, my dear,' replied Ravenscroft handing a coin to the woman.

'Bless you both, and may good fortune go with you.'

Ravenscroft and Lucy continued on their way along the street.

'Now then, which of you Ledbury lads will be brave enough to step up here and take on the Mighty Goliath? Five pounds to anyone who can last two rounds with him,' shouted a bald fat man, dressed in blood-stained shirt and trousers, as he gestured towards a scrawny ugly fellow who was making wild jabbing movements into the air.

'You must be having us on!' replied one of the young men from the crowd of laughing onlookers. 'He looks as though he wouldn't last five seconds!'

'Then you will be taking him on, sir? How about you as well, sir? Who else wants to try his luck? Step this way, folks, and enter the tent! Only threepence to see the bout!'

'Go on, Daniel, see if you can slay the brute!' shouted out a voice.

'Let's see what is further down the street,' suggested Ravenscroft, guiding Lucy away from the excited crowd.

'Step inside now, ladies and gentlemen. Only twopence to see Florinda the famous Bearded Lady, and Gerome the Italian Midget Extraordinaire!' urged a tall showman, smiling as he waved a large red hat in the air.

'Do you wish to see these curiosities?' laughed Ravenscroft.

'I certainly do not.'

'Let us see what that fellow is all about over there. He seems to have attracted quite a large crowd,' said Ravenscroft moving across to where a tall white-bearded man, wearing a striped suit and sporting a bright canary-coloured waistcoat and stovepipe hat, was issuing forth.

'Good evening, ladies and gentlemen! May I introduce myself to you good noble citizens of Ledbury? My name is Silas Lincoln Rockstone, and as you can tell from the colour of my apparel, and the tone of my voice, I am not from these parts. No, sir. I hail from the great city of New York! And you may well all be thinking, what is a fine upstanding gentleman like me doing here tonight? Well, I can tell all you good people of Ledbury. I am on a mission. Oh yes, I am on a mission to save you all!'

'Come, Lucy, I think we have heard enough of this nonsense,' said Ravenscroft turning away from the showman. 'I am not in the mood tonight for any kind of religious conversion.'

'I think he is quite entertaining. Oh, Samuel, do let us stay and see what he has to say,' Lucy implored.

'If you really insist.'

'I have come here tonight not to save your souls, but your bodies!' continued the showman with a dramatic flourish. 'I have heard that the inhabitants of this quaint old English town do not require more of God. No, sir! They are religious enough! I have come here amongst you tonight to cure your ailments and ills. I have heard that this is a sick town. Oh yes! There are people hereabouts who are lying in their beds suffering from all kind of illnesses, coughing and sweating, unable to do a day's honest work without suffering unspeakable agonies and pain. There are young men and women amongst you here tonight who are old before your time. Many of you have numerous aches and pains, being afflicted by weakened bones, while others of you have ugly warts and other unsightly marks that will not disappear. Last month I was in New York when I had a dream. Yes, my friends, a dream. And in my dream a voice called out to me, "Save the good folks of Ledbury. They are a-crying out for relief from their suffering. You must travel across the mighty Atlantic Ocean and help the afflicted." Well, I tell you that help is now at hand to save you, my brothers and sisters. Do not despair. I have come amongst you to cure you all! I have cured the sick and the infirm of New York City, and now I am here amongst you tonight to offer you the divine intervention of Silas Lincoln Rockstone! I have a large bag here that contains all my secret medical remedies. You tell me your complaint and I guarantee that I will have something here that will cure it. Who will be the first to step forward and ask to be cured?'

A silence fell upon the audience.

'Come, now, don't be shy. Who will be bold enough to step forward?'

'I will,' shouted out a youth from the back of the crowd.

'Who calls? Don't be shy. Come forward, young man, and show yourself,' urged the showman.

The crowd parted as the youth came closer towards the small platform upon which the speaker stood.

'Have I not seen you before?'

'Yes, sir. Last week in Bromsgrove.'

'Ah yes, I remember. And what was your complaint?'

'Me face were all covered in boils. Nasty boils; big red horrible boils. They used to itch and burst wide open!' replied the youth with dramatic effect, as several members of the audience exclaimed.

'And how many of these boils were there?' asked the showman intently.

'Ten, sir,' replied the youth somewhat hesitantly.

'Ten boils! But I can see no boils now. Where are your boils?' asked the man looking down seriously at the youth.

'All gone, sir.'

'All gone! And why have these boils gone?'

'Because of the ointment, sir.'

'Ah, the ointment — and from whom did you acquire this miraculous medication?'

'Why, from you, sir.'

'Was this the ointment?' Rockstone reached into a large black bag that had been positioned on a stool at his side, and bringing forth up a small green jar, as some members of the audience gasped.

'Yes, sir.'

'So you purchased this ointment from me but seven days ago, and you followed my instructions?'

'Yes, sir. I rubbed the cream on my face twice a day as you said, sir.'

'Step up here, my good man,' instructed Rockstone. 'Let me look at your face. I can see no boils. Turn to face my friends. Let them gaze upon you. Can any of you see any boils on this man's face?'

Loud muttering in the audience as the throng began to edge forwards.

'Now I will give a shiny sixpence to anyone here tonight who can see a boil on this man's face,' challenged the show-man, peering at his audience through his large spectacles.

Again the crowd moved even closer to the platform.

'I am cured!' shouted the young man, flinging his arms so wildly into the air that the front row of the crowd recoiled.

'Do you hear that, my friends? This man has been cured, in only seven days!' shouted Rockstone, triumphantly brandishing the youth's arm. 'And how much did you pay, sir, for this miracle?'

'Threepence, sir.'

'Only threepence! A small price to pay for such a mir-acle! Thank you, my good man. You may now step down.

Now, which of you here would care to purchase a bottle of my preparation? Not only will it banish boils for ever, but it will also remove spots, warts and smallpox scars, even unsightly birth marks. Apply twice a day to the disfigured area and I can guarantee that within a week your afflictions will be a thing of the past. Thank you kindly, sir. Thank you, madam. You will not regret your investment, I can assure you. Thank you. Thank you.'

'What nonsense,' said Ravenscroft to his wife as they watched the showman handing over his jars of ointment to eager members of his audience.

'Can't you arrest him?' asked Lucy. 'The man is clearly making false claims for his miracle cream.'

'What for? If the fools want to part with their money, who am I to prevent them?'

'Thank you, folks, most kindly. Now what else can I help you with? Aching backs? Noisy coughs? Dizzy spells? I have just the thing here,' continued the American.

'I would like some of Doctor Gazzey's Wonder Pills,' shouted out Ravenscroft from the back of the crowd.

The showman paused for a moment as he peered into the audience trying to ascertain who had asked the question.

'Do you have any of Doctor Gazzey's Wonder Pills?' repeated Ravenscroft.

'Who asks?' enquired a hesitant Rockstone.

'A friend of mine has recently taken some of Doctor Gazzey's pills,' continued Ravenscroft as a hush descended on the audience. 'I wondered whether you had some for me to purchase?'

'I do indeed.' The showman reached once more into his bag. 'I think this is what you are looking for. Guaranteed to cure all ills and revive the tired constitution, as well as put a smile on your good lady's face.'

Lucy blushed as several members of the crowd laughed.

'I would seek a quiet word with you, sir,' requested Ravenscroft, moving closer to the platform.

'Gentleman requires a quiet word with me. What can that be about!' exclaimed Rockstone as more laughter broke out in the audience. 'We cannot keep the lady waiting, can we?'

Ravenscroft leaned forward and whispered into the man's ear. 'I am a police officer.'

Rockstone's eyes widened. 'Right. I see. Okay, folks, that's all for now.' There were loud groans from the audience.

'Perhaps we could go somewhere more private?' suggested Ravenscroft.

'If you and your good lady would care to follow me, sir, into the tent over there, I am sure we will not be disturbed,' said the American, quickly recovering his composure.

Ravenscroft and Lucy followed him across the street and into a small bell tent which had been erected in front of one of the buildings.

'Now, before your seek to question me about my remedies, I can assure you that I am a graduate of the finest university in New York City, and that I can produce a long list of patients who can vouch for the effectiveness of my cures. Why, you saw now how that youth has been saved from his terrible affliction. You will find nothing wrong with my medicines and ointments,' declared Rockstone, speaking in a quick manner before Ravenscroft could utter a word.

'Did I do alright, Mr Rockstone?' asked a figure suddenly parting the flaps of the tent.

Ravenscroft recognised the youth who had spoken up at the gathering.

'Go away! Can't you see I am busy?' growled the showman.

'An acquaintance of yours?' smiled Ravenscroft.

'I can see that you are a man of this world. You have no doubt purchased such medicines in the past, and can see that they cause no harm.' Smiling, Rockstone placed his hand on Ravenscroft's shoulder.

'That is a matter for debate. All I can see, sir, is that you are a charlatan, seeking to separate the good citizens of Ledbury from their hard-earned savings.'

'Come now, I seek to deceive no one. My cures have been tested on many people, with great success. Why, there are thousands in New York City who are leading better lives today thanks to one or more of my medicines. Why even the President of the United States and his good wife have benefitted from my expertise. You would surely not deprive the good folks of Ledbury from receiving the care and attention that they all need?' replied Rockstone in his defence.

'It is a wicked act to deprive honest people of their savings,' declared Lucy indignantly.

'You have proof of that accusation, madam?'

'I have not come here tonight to enquire into the medicinal properties of your so-called cures,' said Ravenscroft. 'All I seek from you is some information.'

'Information?'

'Yes. I presume that Doctor Gazzey's Wonder Pills are one of your creations?'

'They are indeed, and proud I am of them.'

'Have you sold many boxes of these pills recently?'

'Not for several weeks. I am waiting for a new supply to be shipped over from New York.'

'Why would a person wish to purchase such an item? What ailment would you seek to cure them of?' enquired Ravenscroft.

'Whatever concerned them at the time: fatigue, aching bones, laxity, increased circulation, general well-being,' replied Rockstone proudly.

'I must confide in you,' said Ravenscroft, drawing nearer. 'I am at present investigating a murder.'

'A murder!'

'Rather an unpleasant one at that. Just over two weeks ago a man was found hanging from a tree situated in the Malvern Hills. Despite extensive police enquiries we have been unable to identify the victim, but inside his pocket was a small box containing your pills.'

'I see. And you are Sergeant —?'

'I am Inspector Ravenscroft, of the local constabulary.'

'Inspector Ravenscroft,' repeated an uneasy Rockstone. 'Pray, Inspector, would you be able to describe this unfortunate man?'

'I can indeed, Mr Rockstone. He was aged around thirty, with a ruddy brown complexion, probably of the labouring classes although his hands were not excessively worn. He had a small scar on his left cheek.'

'Oh my lord!' exclaimed the salesman, bringing his hand up to his forehead.

'You know the gentleman?' asked Ravenscroft hopefully.

'Indeed I do. It is Jacob. Poor Jacob!'

'Jacob, you say? I presume that was his Christian name? You know his last name?'

'No, no, we knew him only as Jacob.'

'When did you last see this man?'

'About three weeks ago. The fair was in Hereford at the time. He just left one night without any warning. He just left.'

'Was Jacob employed by you, or by the fair?'

'Both.'

'What kind of work was he engaged in?'

'He helped generally with the fair, assisting with the setting up and taking down of the various tents and booths, advertising the fair in towns before our arrival, driving the wagons, helping run the stalls, that kind of thing. The reason he may have had the box of pills in his pocket was because he would often produce them when I . . . er . . . address the crowds,' stuttered Rockstone.

'You mean that he was usually the person in the audience who claimed he had been cured?' smiled Ravenscroft.

'I find that members of the public are somewhat reticent in coming forward. If they can see however that one of their number has been cured, they are more inclined to do so. It is all quite legal. It is merely a little mild entertainment. It does no harm.'

'How long had this Jacob been in the fair's employment?'

'Nearly two years.'

'Where did you first meet Jacob?'

'In New York City.'

'So he is American?' asked Lucy.

'Oh no, madam. He was English.'

'And what was he doing in New York?' Ravenscroft was anxious to know more about the unfortunate man.

'I have no idea. He never said. I remember he just came to the fair one day and enquired if he could seek employment with us.'

'Tell me, Mr Rockstone, when did the fair leave New York and come to England?'

'About six months ago.'

'Was Jacob happy to be returning to the country of his birth?'

'If he was, he did not show it. He seemed quite indifferent.'

'When you and your colleagues came to England which part of the country did you travel to?'

'Rather a strange question, Inspector.'

'Nevertheless, I would be grateful if you would answer it.'

'The fair first travelled around the villages near London, then north towards Manchester and then west to North Wales.'

'And during these travels did Jacob ever speak about where he might have originated from?'

'No, I believe not,' answered the puzzled showman. 'But I do remember that just before we set off for Hereford he became very upset, saying that he believed the fair would do no good there, and that we should go to South Wales instead.'

'That is all very interesting. And you say that the fair did go to Hereford, and that was when he left suddenly?'

'That is correct, Inspector. I was addressing a large crowd there, and was waiting for Jacob to cry out from the audience, but he never appeared. It was all most unsettling.'

'During all the time you knew this Jacob, he never told you his last name, nor spoke of his former life in this country?' asked Ravenscroft, deep in thought.

'That was so.'

'Did you not find that odd?'

'Some people are like that. They want to forget the past. In my profession we learn not to ask too many questions.'

'Indeed. Just one more question. When Jacob left, did he take any of his personal effects with him?'

'No, that was the strange thing. He left all his belongings behind. It was almost as though something frightened him, and he wanted to get away in a hurry.'

'Do you still have any of those personal items?'

'I am afraid not. There was nothing of any value, just some old clothes. We discarded those after a few days, when the fair moved on, and when it seemed that he was not going to return.'

'There were no letters, books, inscribed watches, anything like that?'

'No, there was nothing of that nature.'

'You are certain on that point?'

'Of course,' replied Rockstone, turning away.

'I do not believe you. I find it extraordinary that a man can disappear without any kind of warning, leaving his possessions behind him, and yet you say you found nothing of a personal nature.'

'I have told you that I have nothing that belonged to Jacob,' protested Rockstone.

'And I tell you that you are lying to us. If I call out now, Mr Rockstone, I can summon three policemen into this tent, and not only will we make a thorough search of your person and your effects, but we will also make sure that the fair is closed down immediately, and that you are your colleagues are driven out of the three counties. I trust I make my intentions clear on that point?'

'You do indeed, Inspector. There was this.' Rockstone reluctantly reached into his coat pocket. 'I was of course keeping it in case Jacob returned.'

Ravenscroft accepted a small silver locket and chain, which the showman placed in his hand. 'It would have saved us all a great deal of trouble if you had given this to me earlier in our conversation. Let us see what is inside: a miniature of a young woman. What do you make of it, my dear?'

'What a beautiful picture,' said Lucy after taking the locket from her husband. 'And the subject is certainly a beauty. Her name appears to be Maria, according to the writing opposite.'

'Did Jacob ever speak of this item, or of the lady depicted?' asked Ravenscroft.

'No. I only found the item when I was clearing out his effects.'

'I shall need to take possession of the locket while we make further investigations,' said the detective.

'Of course, Inspector, I understand. Now we know that poor Jacob will not be returning, I can no longer justify retaining the item.'

'Before we leave, Mr Rockstone, I would be obliged if you would tell me your future movements, in case I need to contact you again.'

'Yes, Inspector. We have two more nights here, then the fair travels next to Tewkesbury, where we will be until the end of the week. Next week I believe we will be going on to the town of Evesham, and then to Chipping Norton.'

'May I give you my card? Should you remember anything further concerning Jacob, I would be grateful if you would contact me,' instructed Ravenscroft. He and Lucy made to leave.

'Certainly, Inspector. I will make enquiries of the other fair people to see if Jacob confided in them.'

'I am much obliged to you.'

'Jacob may have been of a rather reserved temperament, but he was a pleasant enough fellow. I hope that you are successful in apprehending his killer.'

'I can assure you we will endeavour to obtain justice for poor Jacob,' said Ravenscroft as he and Lucy took their leave.

CHAPTER TWO

LEDBURY AND CIRENCESTER

'Well, Tom, what do you think of that?'

Ravenscroft had just recounted the events at the fair, as he and Tom Crabb sat in Ledbury Police Station early the following morning.

'That Rockstone fellow sounds quite a charlatan. Do you think he was telling you the truth about this man Jacob?'

'I am not sure. He was certainly reluctant to admit that he was in possession of this locket. I have no doubt he would have sold or pawned it, after a suitable time had elapsed, possibly when he had returned to America. Mr Rockstone makes his living from selling quack potions and ointments, and promises his unfortunate victims that they will be cured of all their ills. By the time they discover that their miracle cure is nothing of the sort, Rockstone and his companions have moved on to some other location. Rockstone said that Jacob was his stooge in the audience, and that his job was to produce Gazzey's Wonder Pills, or some other fake medicine, at the appropriate moment, and then claim that he had been cured. However when the fair was at Hereford Jacob did not perform his role that evening. Something, or someone, must have frightened him so much, that he fled as quickly as he could, not even pausing to pick up his possessions.'

'He could have been kidnapped by the same people who later decided to hang him from that tree on Hangman Hill?' suggested Crabb.

'You could be correct, but either way we know that Jacob did not want the fair to come to Hereford, which means that he was afraid of something happening to him there. Perhaps he previously lived in the area, did someone a great wrong, and fled as a consequence, eventually turning up in New York some years later.'

'And the lady?'

'You mean this "Maria", the subject depicted inside this locket? She obviously meant a lot to Jacob, if he carried her image around with him.'

'Perhaps the lady was his former sweetheart?'

'Or another member of his family; a sister perhaps, or even his mother. She is certainly an attractive woman, quite a beauty, although you had better not tell Mrs Ravenscroft that I have just said that. I wonder who she was, and when the portrait was executed? There is no way of telling, but it is certainly a fine piece of work. Unfortunately we are no closer to finding out who this Jacob really was, and where he came from.'

'Rockstone could have been making the whole thing up. He could have killed Jacob?'

'Yes there is that possibility, but if that was the case, why would he have gone to all the trouble of travelling out to Hangman Hill, and killing his victim there, when there are easier ways to kill a man in Hereford? Hangman Hill. It is so out of the way, it is almost as though Jacob had to be hanged on Hangman Hill, rather than anywhere else. Whatever the man's past, that place had a special significance for his killer or killers.'

'What next then, sir?' asked Crabb.

'I don't know, Tom.' Ravenscroft stared at the portrait in the locket. 'If only we could identify the lady. Give me your pocketknife. It appears as though this miniature has been mounted inside the case since the time it was painted. I wonder, if I tried to lift the portrait from its setting in the locket might there be something on the back?'

Crabb handed over his knife and Ravenscroft gently placed the blade at the edge of the portrait. 'There. Now let's see. There is a small rather faded artist's signature at the bottom, on the reverse. Give me the magnifying glass. I can just make out a name. "Louis Thermaine."'

'He sounds French to me.'

'If we can find out more about this Thermaine, we might then be able to identify the young lady in the portrait, and that in turn may enable us to find out more about our victim.' Ravenscroft replaced the portrait inside the locket.

'How would we do that, sir?' asked Crabb.

'I am not sure. Yes, of course! Come on, Tom. I think I know just the man who may be able to help us,' said Ravenscroft, eagerly rising from his chair.

* * *

Thirty minutes later the two policemen were standing outside a large building, situated at the end of Belle Vue Terrace, in the nearby town of Great Malvern.

'I think Mr Clifford, the proprietor of the Malvern Library and Reading Rooms, may prove of assistance to us,' said Ravenscroft pushing open the door.

'Good morning to you, sir. Why, it is Inspector Ravenscroft if I am not mistaken,' said an immaculately dressed gentleman, who was standing behind a large oak counter. 'And Constable Crabb.'

'Mr Clifford, it is good to make your acquaintance again,' smiled Ravenscroft, removing his hat.

'I trust you are both well, gentlemen?' enquired Clifford. 'It has been some years since you last visited my establishment.'

'Five years I believe,' offered Ravenscroft.

'As long as that? At the time of all those terrible murders that were taking place in Malvern, if I am not mistaken.'

'Yes, you are correct. You were able then to assist us in our enquiries. We now find ourselves requiring your assistance once again, if you would be so kind, Mr Clifford.'

'I would be delighted. How may I be of help?'

'We are seeking information concerning a certain Louis Thermaine.'

'Thermaine, you say? The name is not familiar to me. I do not believe that he could be a resident of the town, or I would have heard of the gentleman.'

'He was an artist,' said Crabb.

'Have you any books in your collection which might provide information regarding such a profession? In particular, he painted miniatures,' said Ravenscroft.

'In what period did this artist flourish? Was he an Elizabethan or medieval artist?' asked Clifford turning round and running his finger along one of the shelves of books on the wall.

'I do not think he was alive then. He was painting some twenty or thirty years ago. We do not know whether he is still alive today.'

'Then I do not think I can be of assistance to you gentlemen. All my reference works contain information concerning earlier artists. No work in my possession contains information regarding current artists. Now, had your man been a member of the aristocracy I am sure we would have found him in either *Who's Who* or *Burke's Peerage*.'

'I see.' Ravenscroft tried to hide his disappointment.

'However, all may not be lost, Inspector. There are the county volumes of The Post Office Directory, which may be of assistance to you. Should your man still be in the land of the living, he could well be listed in one of those volumes. If you would care to follow me, gentlemen.' Clifford led them into an inner room. 'Would you happen to know in which part of the country your Mr Thermaine might be residing?'

'I am afraid not,' answered Ravenscroft.

'Then there is nothing else for it. You will have to go through each county volume in turn,' said Clifford taking down some of the books, and handing one each to the two detectives. 'I suggest that you look under both Artists and also in the Court section.'

'At least our man has a somewhat unusual name,' said Ravenscroft, seating himself at one of the tables.

'That will certainly be of great help to you. Now if you will excuse me, I must attend to the gentleman and lady who have just entered the building,' said Clifford.

'Thank you, Mr Clifford, you have been most helpful,' said Ravenscroft as the librarian left the room.

Several minutes of silence elapsed as the two men turned over the pages of a number of the volumes.

'We don't appear to be having much success,' said a frustrated Ravenscroft. 'That was the last volume in the series.'

'Ah, I believe I may have found the gentleman!' exclaimed Crabb.

Ravenscroft stood up and looked eagerly over his constable's shoulder.

'Well done, Tom. Louis Thermaine is listed as a resident of Cecily Hill in the Gloucestershire market town of Cirencester,' said Ravenscroft adjusting his spectacles to obtain a better view of the writing. 'I wonder if he is also listed under Artists?'

'It would appear not,' replied Crabb, examining the relevant section.

'Perhaps he no longer practises as an artist,' suggested Ravenscroft. 'In the absence of anyone else of the same name, I believe it is worth following up this line of enquiry. As this is the only information we have uncovered in this case, I will have to journey over to Cirencester and see if I can pay this gentleman a visit. If he is still alive then he may be able to name the subject in the locket, and she in turn might be able to tell us more about the man Jacob.'

'What would you like me to do while you are away, sir?' asked Crabb.

'Go and interview as many of the fair people as you can. See if anyone can tell us more about Jacob. He must have confided in someone. Now, there is just one more volume I need to consult,' said Ravenscroft looking at the books on the shelves. 'Yes here we are — Bradshaws. I cannot think that there is a direct train route from Great Malvern to Cirencester. Yes, just as I thought — I must change trains at Worcester and Gloucester. These journeys are never easy.'

* * *

Later that morning Ravenscroft stood in the wide open market place of the Gloucestershire market town of Cirencester, admiring the ancient church with its tall steeple and ornate carvings round its main entrance. He had just visited the local police station, where the officer on duty had informed him that the man he sought was still a resident of the town.

Following the directions he had been given, Ravenscroft made his way along the narrow streets, before turning into a wide avenue, where a collection of fine honey-coloured houses stood on either side of the dusty road, and the entrance to a large park could be glimpsed in the distance. Arriving at one of the houses in the middle of the avenue, he tugged on the bell-pull and was rewarded by the opening of the door by a middle-aged woman dressed in a servant's attire.

'Good morning. I would like to speak with Monsieur Thermaine.' Ravenscroft smiled at the maid as he removed his hat.

'Do you have an appointment, sir?'

'No, but it is essential that I speak with Monsieur Thermaine,' began Ravenscroft.

'Then I am afraid you cannot see the master. He will only see people by appointment,' replied the sour-faced maid beginning to close the door.

'I have come upon most urgent business,' interjected Ravenscroft, placing his hand on the woodwork. 'I have come on important police business. It is imperative that I see Monsieur Thermaine. If you would give my card to your master, I would be obliged. Tell him that I only require a few minutes of his time.'

The maid took the card and studied it for several seconds.

'It really is most urgent,' stressed Ravenscroft.

'I will see what the master has to say. Wait there,' snapped the unsmiling maid, quickly closing the door in Ravenscroft's face.

Ravenscroft took out his pocket watch, looked casually around at the other buildings in the street, and then up at the heavily curtained windows of the artist's residence, before walking impatiently up and down the pavement.

As the seconds turned into minutes, and the door firmly closed in front of him, he found himself becoming more and more anxious. To have come so far, with only the most tentative of possibilities open to him, and to be denied entry at this time, was an outcome that was not to be borne.

After a further two minutes had elapsed, Ravenscroft reached out for the bell-pull once more, just as the door suddenly opened before him.

'Master will see you now, but only for a few minutes.'

'I am much obliged.' Somewhat relieved, Ravenscroft stepped into the hallway.

'Follow me,' instructed the maid, in a tone which Ravenscroft did not consider as entirely hospitable.

The maid tapped loudly on one of the doors at the end of a badly lit passageway that Ravenscroft observed was lined with paintings.

'Enter,' cried out a cracked voice from within.

Ravenscroft stepped into a small, darkened, almost airless room, where the only light came from the hearth and a solitary candle.

'Ravenscroft, it says here,' said a frail voice.

'Yes. I trust I have the honour of addressing Monsieur Louis Thermaine, the distinguished artist?' replied Ravenscroft as he edged tentatively towards a small, heavily wrinkled man, who was seated in an armchair situated before an almost burnt out fire.

'You had better sit down there.' Thermaine pointed a long thin bony finger towards a wooden chair.

'I will endeavour not to take up too much of your time,' said Ravenscroft, accepting the seat.

'I can give you five minutes,' grumbled Thermaine. Ravenscroft wondered why time was important to him, when he had not appeared to have been engaged in any fruitful activity when he had entered the room.

'I would be grateful if you would look at this locket for me,' said Ravenscroft, taking the item from out of his coat pocket.

The old man stared at Ravenscroft for several seconds, before reaching out to accept the item.

'Give me that candle, on the table there.'

Ravenscroft turned around, picked up the candlestick and passed it over to Thermaine, who accepted it with an unsteady hand. As the flickering flame drew nearer to the artist's face Ravenscroft observed the thin paper-like skin, yellow complexion and haunted look in his eyes.

'You came by train?'

'Indeed.'

Thermaine coughed but said nothing as Ravenscroft cast his eyes around the room. Two or three items of medi-ocre continental porcelain stood at either end of the mantle over the fireplace. A faded photograph in a damaged frame assumed a lonely role on the opposite wall, and a ragged stuffed owl looked out at him from beneath a glass dome on an adjoining table. He wondered why the artist had chosen to furnish his room with such unappealing items.

The artist coughed again but said nothing as he studied the locket intently. Ravenscroft was relieved when he at last broke the silence.

'I have never seen this before. I do not know why you have come here today.'

'If you would care to open the locket, I believe you may discover something of interest,' urged Ravenscroft.

Thermaine stared at Ravenscroft again for several seconds, then turning his attention towards the locket opened the covering to the case. 'Where did you get this?'

'I am making enquiries concerning the death of a man in the Malvern Hills, three weeks ago. He went by the Christian name of Jacob. The locket was one of his possessions.'

'This is of no interest to me,' retorted the other, suddenly snapping the lid shut and turning away to face the dying embers in the fireplace.

'I have come here today because your name appears on the reverse of the miniature. I believe you may have painted this portrait? The sitter would appear to be called Maria,' continued Ravenscroft, somewhat at a loss for the artist's unhelpful attitude.

'I cannot help you. You had better go,' said Thermaine.

'Then you are not the artist of this work?'

'Why do you want to know that for? It is a long time since I was engaged in such activity. I have no interest in painting now.'

'Jacob was murdered in a brutal fashion. We know nothing about him, except for the fact that this locket appears to have been his most prized possession. If I am to apprehend his killer, I must know more about him. I ask you again, sir, to take another look at this miniature, and tell me what you know about the lady,' urged Ravenscroft anxiously.

'I have not undertaken any commissions for the past fifteen years. My eyes, they are not what they were,' muttered Thermaine.

'I wonder whether you used to live in Paris?' asked Ravenscroft, realising that he would have to change the subject if he was to obtain any useful information from the artist.

'Who told you that?'

'You are French, and I assumed that you may have once resided there.'

'The Commune!' exclaimed Thermaine suddenly sitting upright and staring at Ravenscroft in a wild fashion.

'The Paris Commune. 1871. I remember reading about it at the time,' replied Ravenscroft taken aback by the sudden change in Thermaine's manner and wondering what he should say.

'They killed my friends, you know. I went back to save them, but I was too late,' said the artist as tears began to form in his eyes.

'It must have been terrible for you,' said Ravenscroft sympathetically after a moment's silence had elapsed.

'They murdered the women and children,' continued Thermaine sadly. 'Why did they do that? Will you tell me why? You have no comprehension of the situation we found ourselves in. Why? My poor wife, they showed her no mercy.'

'I am sorry. You said you went back to Paris. Were you living in England before you returned to Paris?' asked Ravenscroft.

'Yes, but what is it to you?'

'That must have been difficult — I mean, starting anew in a foreign country?'

The artist said nothing as he slumped back into his chair.

'When did you first arrive in England?'

'In 1860.'

'Where did you first go to, when you came to England? London?'

'There was nothing for me there. I went to Bristol for a while, then Hereford, before coming here to Cirencester.'

'You mentioned Hereford,' said Ravenscroft eagerly. 'How long were you in Hereford?'

'I was there only for a few months. There was little work for me to undertake. The people there were all philistines. Philistines, I tell you.'

'You undertook commissions while in Hereford?'

'Enough!' exclaimed Thermaine, almost throwing the locket into Ravenscroft's lap before drawing a large shawl around his shoulders. 'I have answered enough of your silly questions. I want you to go now. I am tired.'

'And you can tell me nothing regarding the lady depicted in the portrait?' asked Ravenscroft, replacing the locket in his coat pocket as he stood up.

The old man said nothing, gesturing with his arm that Ravenscroft should leave, before blowing out the candle.

'It is most important that I know her name.'

Thermaine remained silent, staring into the dying embers before him.

Ravenscroft paused for a few seconds, hoping that Thermaine would say more, but eventually realising that he could obtain no further information from the artist he made his way out of the room, where he found the maid waiting to escort him to the front entrance of the building.

'How long has it been since your master gave up painting?' he asked, straining to see the many portraits that adorned the walls of the dimly lit passageway.

'Master does not paint any more. What business is it of yours?' muttered the servant woman.

'These are fine portraits. This one in particular is most interesting,' said Ravenscroft, intently studying the portrait which hung nearest the outer door.

'You should go. Master is not well. He is not long for this world. You should not come again. He does not like to be bothered.'

Ravenscroft took out the locket from his pocket and looked down at the miniature before casting a final glance at the portrait on the wall.

'Thank you,' smiled Ravenscroft, stepping out into the street. 'I believe I may now have all the information I need.'

CHAPTER THREE

THE VERZONS

'Maria Constantine!' proclaimed Ravenscroft after he had narrated the morning's events to Crabb, back in Ledbury.

'Forgive me, sir, but I thought you said that Thermaine denied all knowledge of the miniature?' asked a puzzled Crabb.

'He did, but it seems that he not only painted miniatures, but that he also made larger versions of his work. They were all hanging in his entrance hall, and one of them I recognised as the lady in the locket. Fortunately a small label at the bottom of the portrait bore the name "Maria Constantine."'

'That was most fortunate.'

'Indeed, Tom. I cannot make up my mind whether Thermaine recognised the painting in the locket and for some reason did not want me to know who she was, or whether he genuinely had no recollection of her. Either way, I suppose it does not matter. As you say, Tom, it was indeed fortunate that I saw the larger portrait.'

'If Thermaine came to this county in 1860, why did he then go back to Paris in 1870, when the city was in a state of civil war?'

'Yes, I must say I do find that rather extraordinary. I wish he had told me more about those troubled times. He did say his wife had been killed during the time of the Commune. I wonder if she had been left behind when Thermaine came over here in 1860, and that he then returned ten years later to try and save her?'

'It seems rather strange to me, to leave one's wife in one country, while you go to another, and then you go back ten years later. I know that Mrs Crabb would never entertain such an idea.'

'Nor Mrs Ravenscroft, either. No, I feel there is another mystery waiting to be unravelled there, but I am not sure that the solving of it would assist us in finding out more about the poor man murdered on Hangman Hill. The whole thing could have been mere ramblings by an old fantasist. I think we should leave Monsieur Thermaine for the present, and concentrate all our efforts on finding this Maria Constantine. We know that Jacob was afraid of returning to this area, and we also now know that Thermaine first came to Hereford when he arrived in this country in 1860, if the old man's memory is to be believed. He probably set up a studio of some sort in the city where he no doubt advertised his services as an artist, hoping to secure commissions from the gentry. Maria Constantine must have been one of his clients,' said Ravenscroft, staring at the miniature in the locket.

'That would make the portrait just over thirty years old.'

'Yes, Tom. Maria must have been around twenty, when the commission was undertaken. She would be around fifty years of age by now, if she is still alive.'

'Constantine could have been her maiden name,' suggested Crabb.

'If that is the case then we will have no chance of finding her.'

'Unless the lady never married.'

'You could be right, Tom. Pass me the Herefordshire Post Office Directory. There is just a remote possibility that we might discover her still listed within its pages.'

Crabb searched through the row of books on the shelf in the corner of the room of the police station.

'It's two years out of date.'

'Never mind, it may give us the information we require,' said Ravenscroft turning over the pages of the red volume. 'Ah, here we are. "Mr Francis Constantine. Miss Maria Constantine. The Verzons, Ashperton." Good Lord, that is only about five or six miles or so from here.'

'I've seen that Verzons. It is that large house on the side of the road, just before you reach the crossroads at Trumpet,' said Crabb.

'I know the one you mean. We must have passed by it several times on our way to Hereford. Quickly, Tom, get the trap. We shall proceed with all haste. This may be the vital information we seek. I just hope that Maria Constantine is still alive, and that she can identify the locket as once having belonged to her.'

* * *

Crabb turned the trap off the main road, and into the court-yard of the large Georgian house.

'A fine building,' remarked Ravenscroft, as he stepped out of the horse-drawn vehicle.

'I think someone has noticed our arrival,' said Crabb.

Ravenscroft turned to see a ruddy-faced, stout middle-aged man, wearing a tweed suit and waistcoat, walking towards them, a large sheepdog at his side. 'Good day to you, sir. I believe this to be the Verzons?'

'You are correct, sir,' answered the man.

'I am looking for Mr Francis Constantine.'

'Well you've found him.'

'I understand that a Miss Maria Constantine also resides here?'

'She does. She is my sister,' replied Francis Constantine, giving Ravenscroft a suspicious look.

'Excellent. My name is Ravenscroft. I am a detective police inspector in Ledbury.'

'I know who you are.'

'I see. This is my colleague, Constable Crabb. I would be obliged if you and your sister could give us a few moments of your time.'

'What for?' asked the landowner bluntly.

'I would prefer to speak with both you and your sister, if I may.'

'I can't think why.'

'It is a matter of great importance, I can assure you,' persisted Ravenscroft.

'You'd best come in, then. Stay, Brutus!' commanded Constantine, addressing the sheepdog, which lay down in the yard as its owner led the way through the main entrance of the building.

'Where's your mistress?' Constantine enquired of a young maid who came running towards the door.

'In the parlour, sir,' replied the maid.

'Follow me, gentlemen,' instructed Constantine.

Ravenscroft and Crabb followed the landowner through to a small room. A woman sat at the table, her back towards them. She appeared to be engaged in undertaking some kind of needlework.

'Police to see us,' said Constantine.

The woman stood up, and as she turned, Ravenscroft realised that he had found the woman he was seeking. Although her face was now lined and aged, it had nevertheless retained the same beauty, elegance and mystery that the artist had captured in her portrait.

'Says his name is Ravenscroft, and that he must speak with both of us,' continued Constantine. 'He's the police from Ledbury.'

'Inspector Ravenscroft,' answered the woman, somewhat startled by the unexpected arrivals.

'Forgive the intrusion, Miss Constantine,' replied Ravenscroft somewhat hesitantly, as he realised that he was staring at his hostess. 'I am Detective Inspector Ravenscroft, and this is Constable Crabb.'

36

'You had better take a seat, gentlemen. Perhaps you would care for some tea?'

'No, thank you. That will not be necessary,' replied Ravenscroft looking round the room, which seemed to him to emit both a comfort and keen attention to detail, which its owner must have carefully bestowed upon it over the years. It almost resembled a kind of sanctuary, a retreat from the outside world.

'Now then, Ravenscroft, I hope you have not come about my sheepdogs. That confounded fellow down the road, Martin, is always complaining; nothing better to do with his time.'

'No, Mr Constantine, it is not about your dogs.'

'Always complaining about the dogs, he is; the man is an interfering busybody. Don't know why he can't just leave people alone,' muttered the farmer.

'I would be obliged, Miss Constantine, if you would take a look at this for me,' said Ravenscroft ignoring her brother's remarks as he passed over the locket.

'Oh my God!' exclaimed Maria Constantine, turning a deathly white as she opened the locket.

'What is it?' asked her brother, peering over her shoulder at the open locket. 'What is it that ails you, Maria?'

'I would be grateful if you would confirm that you are the same "Maria" depicted in the locket?' asked Ravenscroft, observing her closely.

'Good grief!' exclaimed Constantine. 'I remember you having that done in Hereford, all those years ago, by that funny French fellow.'

'Monsieur Louis Thermaine,' said Ravenscroft. 'So you can confirm its identity?'

'Yes, yes,' answered Maria Constantine in scarcely a whisper. Her hands were shaking as she stared down at the portrait.

'Said you lost it in the hay fields, as I recall,' offered Constantine, walking over to the fireplace. 'Fancy it turning up after all this time.'

'Can you confirm that Miss Constantine? When was the locket lost?' asked Ravenscroft.

'Yes. It was lost shortly after I had it commissioned. I think it was in 1861,' answered Maria. 'Where did you find it?'

Ravenscroft hesitated for a moment, seeing the look of fear and distress in her face, and not wanting to break the news of how he can come into possession of the locket.

'Well come on, man, where was it hiding?' asked Francis impatiently.

'What I have to tell you, Miss Constantine, may be very distressing for you to hear. Three weeks ago the body of a man was found hanging from a tree on Hangman Hill in the Malvern Hills,' began Ravenscroft, trying to speak as calmly as he could.

'Good Lord! The poor fellow,' exclaimed Constantine.

'Unfortunately he had been killed in a brutal fashion. At first we were unable to identify him, but by a chance encounter we discovered that he had been travelling with a visiting fair, at present in Ledbury. He went by the name of Jacob. When we made a search of the dead man's possessions we found this locket.'

Maria brought her hands towards her ashen face, as her eyes began to fill with tears.

'There, Maria, don't distress yourself so,' said a startled Constantine placing his hand on his sister's shoulders. 'It's distressing and all that, but don't fret. It is not as though you knew the poor unfortunate fellow.'

'I apologise for any distress caused, Miss Constantine, but can you tell me whether you might have known this man, Jacob? We estimate that he must have been nearly thirty years of age. Apparently he had been working in New York when he joined the fair there.'

'No, no,' answered Maria trying to control her tears as she turned away.

'We've never been to New York, so how would we have known him?' protested the farmer.

'We believe he may have originated from Herefordshire,' said Ravenscroft.

'Jacob, you say? The name means nothing to me.'

'Miss Constantine?' asked Ravenscroft leaning forwards towards the unhappy woman.

'No. No,' she replied in scarcely a whisper.

'Someone must have picked up the locket shortly after you lost it, Maria,' suggested Constantine.

'That is possible. I am sorry to ask you again, but can you confirm that you lost the locket all those years ago? You did not give it to anyone, as a kind of keepsake, or as an act of remembrance?' asked Ravenscroft.

'No. No. It is as my brother has just said. I was foolish enough to lose the locket in one of the fields. It was very clumsy of me.' Maria dabbed her eyes with her handkerchief as she attempted to control her emotions.

'I am sorry to have caused you any distress. I must ask you for the return of the locket, if you will,' said Ravenscroft.

'Surely I may keep it, after all these years,' pleaded Maria looking up into Ravenscroft's eyes.

'I am afraid I must retain it for the present, as it is police evidence, and may be required for further identification. However I am sure that once this case has been brought to a satisfactory conclusion, the locket will be returned to you as its rightful owner.'

Ravenscroft saw the look of deep sadness in Maria Constantine's eyes as she reluctantly returned the locket.

'How long after the portrait was commissioned did you realise that you had lost it?'

'A few months, maybe a year; I cannot remember.'

'Did you ever loan the locket to anyone?'

'No. Why should I?'

'Look, Ravenscroft, all this has been most upsetting for my sister. We have answered your questions. The prodigal locket has returned to the fold. Can't see why you cannot now return it to my sister,' said Constantine.

'Thank you, Miss Constantine. We will take our leave of you,' said Ravenscroft ignoring the farmer's last remarks. 'If either of you can think of anything which will assist us in our investigations, we can be contacted at the police station in Ledbury.'

'I'll show you out,' said Constantine.

* * *

'She is lying to us,' said Ravenscroft as the trap made its way back to Ledbury.

'She certainly went a deathly colour when you produced that locket,' remarked Crabb. 'I thought the poor woman was going to faint.'

'Yes, not the reaction you'd expect. I don't believe that story about losing it in the hay fields all those years ago. I think she gave it to someone, someone who was very dear to her at that time.'

'Jacob would have been an infant at the time.'

'No, it was probably given to someone else. A lover, perhaps?'

'Perhaps she thought, when she saw the locket, that whoever she gave it to had died,' suggested Crabb.

'I believe you are correct, Tom. When she parted with the locket, she must have expected that she would see neither it nor its new owner ever again. To whom did she give it? Why did she want to make us believe that she had lost it in the hay fields all those years ago, a story which her brother also substantiated?'

'She was covering up for something that happened then.'

'Of course, she must have made up the story at the time, and told her brother of her loss — but why? Why did she not tell the truth, and admit that she had given it away?'

'Because she knew that her brother would not approve of her conduct?'

'Indeed. That would explain why she still had to keep up that pretence, even now after all these years. Damn it! Our lives would be much easier if people just told us the truth. Of course,' he added, 'there is another possibility, which we have not yet considered.'

'What is that?'

'That whoever Maria Constantine gave that locket to has either died or mislaid it in the intervening years. Jacob could then have then found the locket, or inherited it from someone, or even stolen it, in which case we are following this case from the wrong direction. Jacob may have had no connection at all with Maria Constantine or Louis Thermaine. It could have been a mere coincidence that the locket was found amongst his effects.'

'But you don't really believe that, sir?'

'No, I don't. There is a connection somewhere between Jacob and Maria Constantine.'

'Could Francis Constantine have killed Jacob?' suggested Crabb.

'To protect his sister, you mean? I cannot see that, but at this stage of our investigation we cannot discount any possibility. If only we knew why Jacob was afraid of returning to this area. And what the devil was he doing in America in the first place? The fair is still in Ledbury for another night; let us have one more attempt before it departs to see if we can obtain any further information about Jacob.'

* * *

The daylight had begun to fade as Ravenscroft and Crabb made their way through the noisy excited crowds who thronged the streets of Ledbury.

'The man who runs the fair is called Evan Walker,' said Crabb.

'Then let us start with him,' replied Ravenscroft.

'That's him over there, on the wheel of fortune.'

'Mr Walker?' said Ravenscroft, walking over towards a heavily built, unshaven, casually dressed showman who was in the process of dealing out some cards to a group of men. 'Might I have a word with you. My name is Detective Inspector Ravenscroft.'

'Your constable there interviewed me earlier today. I've told him all that I knows. Now then, ladies and gentlemen, last cards before we spin the lucky wheel!'

'Nevertheless I would be grateful for a few further minutes of your time. It is a serious matter we are investigating,' persisted Ravenscroft.

'Here we go! Who will be the lucky winner this time?' said Walker, ignoring Ravenscroft as he spun the wheel. 'Ah, sorry, ladies and gentlemen, this would appear not to be your lucky chance.'

'Mr Walker, I must insist,' shouted Ravenscroft above the noise of a group of revellers who nearly collided with him.

'Alright, alright,' grumbled Walker. 'Sorry folks, stall is closed for next few minutes. Blame it on the law.'

'The punters let out cries of disappointment before they drifted reluctantly away.

'Now, what do you want to know?' said the showman drawing himself up to his full height and glaring directly into Ravenscroft's face.

'We understand that the fair was in America last year?'

'No. We have never been to America. Whatever gave you that idea?'

'Mr Rockstone told us that he and Jacob were in America with the fair, before it came to this country.'

'Well Rockstone got it wrong, didn't he?' growled Walker.

'So you were not in America last year?'

'Fair has always been in England.'

'So when did Rockstone and Jacob join the fair?'

'About six months ago.'

'Where did they join?'

'In Birmingham, I think. Look, is this going to take all night? I've got a livelihood to keep up.'

'We won't detain you longer than is necessary Mr Walker. So Rockstone and Jacob joined the fair together?'

'That's what I said.'

'Did Rockstone ever mention New York, or how he had met Jacob?' continued Ravenscroft determined to know more.

'They just said they had recently travelled over from New York. Came over on one of them old Cunard ships they said. They just wanted to join the fair.'

'So you let them?'

'Why should I not? They pays me a fee to be with us, so why should I turn them away?'

'We believe Jacob came from this area.'

'I wouldn't know where he came from.'

'He never mentioned it to you?'

'No. Look, what is all this?' asked Walker becoming more and more red in the face, as his responses grew louder and more aggressive in tone.

'Surely Jacob must have said something about his past?'

'He said nothing. Kept very much to himself, he did. He never said more than a dozen words to me the whole time he were here.'

'We believe that Jacob did not want the fair to go to Hereford. Why was that?'

'First I've heard of this,' snapped the showman.

'According to Mr Rockstone, Jacob was frightened that something would happen to him if the fair came to Hereford.'

'As I've just said, I knew nothing about this.'

'Then we will have to ask Mr Rockstone about this. Where is the gentleman?'

'You won't find him here. He left early this morning.'

'Left this morning!' exclaimed Ravenscroft.

'That's what I said. Have you done? Now let me get on,' replied Walker, turning away.

'He left rather suddenly, didn't he?'

'Folk come and go all the time; it's the nature of the fair business. Roll up, ladies and gentlemen, come and try your luck on the wheel of fortune. There's one whole gold sovereign to be given away tonight to one lucky winner!'

'Did he say where he was going?' Ravenscroft shouted over the noise of the boisterous new arrivals.

'Why would he tell me? Thank you, sir, just twopence a go!'

'Did he leave anything behind?'

'He took everything with him. I thank you, madam; thank you, sir.'

'What about the young man who acted as his stooge in the audience?' asked Crabb.

'He went with him as well. Come on, folks, come and try your luck on the wheel of fortune.'

'Thank you, Mr Walker. Come on, Tom, we can do nothing further here tonight.' Annoyed, Ravenscroft walked away.

'What do we do now, sir?' asked Crabb.

'Issue a description of this Rockstone and send it to all the local police stations. Confound it, Tom. We should have taken him into custody last night!'

CHAPTER FOUR

LEDBURY

'What will you do now?' asked Lucy the following morning, as she and her husband sat together at the breakfast table.

'Try and track down that quack Rockstone. He can't have got far.'

'Do you think he might have killed Jacob? He certainly seemed an unpleasant man.'

'I don't really know, but the fact that he has left the town in a hurry tends to suggest that he knows a lot more about the dead man than he has told us. He may have been responsible for his murder, but if so, I can't see the motive, or why he would have gone to all that trouble of hanging Jacob up on Hangman Hill. There may be another reason for his hasty departure — perhaps he may be a wanted man, and was afraid that if we questioned him further, his past crimes would have come to light. Either way, I do not think this case can proceed until we have apprehended him.' Ravenscroft took another bite of toast.

'He could have left the town by train?' suggested Lucy.

'That is a possibility. After I've finished breakfast I'll take a walk up to the station. If they remember him leaving they might be able to tell me the destination of his ticket. Failing that, Tom and I will go round the local inns to see if he took one of the horses. Then there are the local cabmen to interview; one of them may have taken Rockstone out of town.'

'It seems that you will have quite a busy day. This Maria Constantine sounds quite intriguing.'

'I only wish she had felt inclined to have been more forthcoming concerning that locket. I am sure that she gave it to someone all those years ago, and does not want either her brother, or ourselves, to know who it was.'

'You will have to take her in for more questioning,' suggested Lucy, pouring out another cup of tea.

'I am not sure that would do any good at this stage. I don't think she would tell us anything concerning Jacob and how he might have acquired the locket. She was certainly distressed when I produced it. It obviously meant a great deal to her. I could almost feel her pain and suffering,' said Ravenscroft thoughtfully.

'You are quite taken by this Maria Constantine,' teased Lucy.

'You have nothing to fear on that score. I am utterly devoted to you. But yes, she is certainly an intriguing person, and I would be interested to know more about her. Anyway, we need to track down that charlatan Rockstone, so I will bid you good day, my dear.' Ravenscroft rose from the breakfast table.

'I wish you success with your search.' Lucy smiled as her husband left the room.

* * *

Later that morning Lucy was busily engaged in arranging some flowers on the hall table, when there came a knock on the front door.

'Don't worry, Susan, I'll see to it,' called out Lucy. 'I expect it is only the butcher's boy come about the order.'

Lucy opened the door to discover a middle-aged woman, wearing a long overcoat and shawl, her bonnet pulled low over her face, standing before her.

'Oh, I am sorry to disturb you. I was looking for Inspector Ravenscroft. I have just called at the police station and they thought he might be here,' said the woman somewhat apprehensively.

'I am afraid my husband is away on business at present,' replied Lucy. 'Perhaps you would care to call later?'

'I am afraid I cannot do that. I will call another day,' said the woman quickly turning away.

'Who shall I say has called?'

'It is no matter. I am sorry for the intrusion.' She began to walk away from the cottage.

'Please do not go. You are Miss Constantine, if I am not mistaken. I am Mrs Ravenscroft. Please do come inside,' called out Lucy.

'Yes, I am Maria Constantine,' replied the woman hesitantly. 'How did you know my name?'

'My husband showed me the locket, and mentioned that he had called upon you yesterday.'

'Oh yes, the locket.'

'Do please come inside,' repeated Lucy, hoping that the new arrival would accept her offer.

The woman looked down nervously at her shoes, then followed Lucy inside. 'You are most kind.'

'May I take your bonnet? Do please take a seat. Can I offer you some refreshment?'

'No, thank you. I am sorry for the intrusion.' Maria Constantine seated herself on one of the chairs.

'It is no intrusion, I can assure you.'

'So your husband has told you of his visit to the Verzons yesterday?'

'Yes, he said that he met you and your brother.' Lucy smiled again, hoping that she could put her unsettled guest at her ease.

'I am afraid that I was not very forthcoming in answering your husband's questions; he must have thought me quite rude.'

'My husband is used to asking a great many questions in his line of work.'

'There were things that I could not say in front of my brother,' said Maria.

'I understand.' Lucy had noticed the sadness in the other's eyes.

'Do you? I wonder? Oh, I am sorry, I should not have said that. I did not wish to cause any offence when you have been so kind as to invite me into your home. Perhaps I should go.'

'I can assure you Miss Constantine, that you have not caused any offence.' Lucy placed her hand on the woman's arm. 'I appreciate that it can sometimes be very difficult to talk. I trust that you will stay. I can assure you that whatever you have to tell me will be held in the highest confidence.'

'You are very kind.' Maria stared into Lucy's eyes. 'I believe that you are a woman of this world, and that I may trust you.'

'You have my word.'

'I cannot stay long. My brother is conducting some business in the town, and we are to meet up shortly in the marketplace.'

'Of course, I understand.'

'My story, Mrs Ravenscroft, is not a happy one, and I am now afraid of what the consequences may be, should I be forthcoming in the telling of it. Nevertheless I know that I will not be able to rest until my greatest fears have been confirmed. I am sorry if I am not speaking coherently. Many years ago, I committed a foolish indiscretion.'

Maria Constantine then paused and stared out of the window. Lucy looked down at her hands in her lap, knowing that all she now had to do was to remain silent, until her guest acquired the confidence to continue.

'It was in 1862. I was with child. I could not tell either my parents or my brother. It would have destroyed them.

The scandal, the ruination of our name, our standing in society . . .'

'I understand,' sympathised Lucy, remembering her own previous unhappy circumstances.

'I had to leave the Verzons before others guessed my secret. I made up some pretext about wanting to travel abroad, for several months, with an old school friend of mine. Instead I came to London and rented some rooms in a rather unpleasant boarding house, which provided accommodation for distressed women such as myself. My son was born. He was the most beautiful baby I had ever seen. I named him Christopher.'

'Christopher. That is such a nice name,' said Lucy.

'I thought so as well. He was my son, and I was his mother, and I loved him so, but I knew that I could never take him back to the Verzons. What I did next, I have regretted for every day of my life ever since. I did something quite terrible. I gave away my child to the Foundling Hospital. Please do not judge me too harshly, Mrs Ravenscroft,' implored Maria.

'No, I could never do that,' stuttered Lucy.

'I gave away my darling Christopher!' repeated Maria, the tears beginning to fall from her eyes. 'You are the only person I have ever spoken to about this in all these years. It has been so difficult. It was all I could do at the time. You must see that? I believed the hospital would give my son the start in life that he deserved, and which I could never provide for him. I said to myself that one day, when my parents had died, and my brother was married, I would return and claim back my dear child. That is when I parted with the locket. I gave it to the Hospital as a token. Apparently, that is what the other mothers did, too. They left tokens with the children, so that one day they could return and reclaim that which they had given away. I hoped that as my child grew older he would open that locket, and look down at that portrait, and know that it was his mother there, who loved him so much and who would never forget him.'

Maria paused, and dabbed her eyes with a handkerchief Lucy proffered.

'You do not think that I was cruel?' she suddenly cried out. 'You will judge me for my heartlessness.'

'No. You did what was best at the time.'

'Yes, I have told myself that a great deal over the years, but it has done nothing to assuage my guilt. How can I have been so thoughtless?'

'So you were never able to return to the Foundling Hospital?' asked Lucy after a few moments of silence had elapsed.

'No. My parents died seven and five years ago respectively, my brother had never married during the intervening years, but by then it was too late — my son would have been a man grown by then. At night I would lie awake wondering what had become of him. Perhaps he had become a lawyer, a soldier, a clergyman. Had he become prosperous? Was he now married, with children of his own? I worried that my actions may have blighted his life, and that his future had been cursed by my act of foolishness. How was I to know? Then yesterday your husband visited us at the Verzons, and it seemed that my world had come to an end when he told me of the dead man, and how they had found the locket amongst his possessions!'

'We cannot be sure that the dead man, Jacob, was your son. The locket could have been given to him by your Christopher?' suggested Lucy, hoping to calm the other's fears.

'No, he would never have done that. He would never have given away the locket,' said Maria, pain in her eyes.

'Your son may have lost the locket, and Jacob found it.'

'Do you think so, Mrs Ravenscroft?'

'Please call me Lucy. This man Jacob may not have been your son. Your son could still be alive.'

'Yes, yes, he is still alive. Pray that he is still alive!'

'We just do not know at present. My husband is presently making enquiries concerning a man called Rockstone, an American. Apparently Jacob was working in America, when he met this Rockstone, and that he then sought employment with him.'

'My son went to America?'

'Jacob went to America, but as I said, Miss Constantine, we do not know that Jacob and your son were the same man. All we know at the present is that Rockstone and Jacob travelled over to England, where they joined a travelling fair.'

'A fair? I do not quite understand.'

'Yes, Rockstone was, or rather is, a travelling showman, who sells quack medicines to unsuspecting people, and Jacob was his assistant. Rockstone left the fair in a hurry yesterday, and my husband is desperately trying to find him.'

'I see.' Maria handed back the handkerchief to Lucy.

'I am sure that once my husband has found this Rockstone, he will be able to tell us more about Jacob. More than that, I do not know, Miss Constantine.'

'Maria.'

'Maria. At the present we have no way of knowing whether your son is alive or dead, but I can assure you that I, or rather my husband and I, will do all that is within our power to obtain the truth.'

'You are so very kind Mrs Ravenscroft . . . Lucy.'

'As soon as we know anything you can be certain that we will inform you of the outcome.'

'Thank you . . . but you must not come to the Verzons. I cannot let my brother know the truth. He would never forgive me,' said an anxious Maria rising from her seat.

'Then I shall write.'

'Yes, yes, that would be better.'

'You would have no objection if I told my husband of our meeting?' asked Lucy. 'If we are to locate your son, he must know everything that you have just told me.'

'No, I appreciate what you are saying. You have been so very kind, but I must leave now. My brother will be wondering what has become of me.'

'Maria, perhaps you should talk with your brother. You may find that he is more understanding and sympathetic to your predicament than you had previously thought.'

'No, I could never do that. You would not say that if you knew my brother,' said Maria shaking her head. 'He would become very angry. I know that. He would cast me out.'

'I am sorry. I have been somewhat presumptuous. Maria, rest assured that we will do everything we can to uncover the truth.' Lucy took the other's hands in hers.

'You have been most kind.'

'Have faith.'

* * *

'Confound it, Tom, where has the fellow gone?' said a frustrated Ravenscroft as he walked into the police station in Ledbury later that afternoon. 'The ticket office at the station has no record of Rockstone leaving town by train, the hostelries have no recollection of hiring out a horse to him, and not one of the cab drivers can remember taking a fare with anyone fitting his description. The man cannot just have walked out of town; it is quite a distance to either Hereford or Malvern.'

'Perhaps he met up with someone?' suggested Crabb.

'But who was that person? I suppose there is another possibility.'

'What is that?'

'Rockstone is hiding somewhere locally, in some barn or outhouse, or even out in the woods.'

'He could still be with the fair? Knowing that we were about to return, the fair people may have taken it upon themselves to hide Rockstone.'

'You may be right. We should make a thorough search of the carts and tents tonight, before they leave.' Wearily, Ravenscroft sank into his chair and set his feet on the desk. 'Take a seat, Tom. The fair can wait for a few minutes.'

'Thank you, sir,' said Crabb gratefully.

'What the deuce!' Ravenscroft suddenly exclaimed. 'The drawer of this desk has been forced open!'

Crabb hurried round to inspect the damage.

'See here, Tom, there are the marks where someone has inserted a sharp implement to force open the lock on the drawer.'

'There was nothing of value in there,' said Crabb.

'Only the photographs of the dead man. They have been taken!'

'Shall I have a look round and see if anything else has been taken?'

'You can, but I think we will find that it is only the photographs that have been removed. Somebody wanted to stop us having any record of Jacob, and what he looked like.'

'Well we cannot take any more photographs,' said Crabb. 'We buried him two weeks ago in that plot in Little Malvern churchyard.'

'Exactly. By stealing our only photographic record of Jacob, they have closed off a useful avenue of investigation.'

'There might still be the original photographic plates?' suggested Crabb. 'We could make further copies.'

'Of course. Who took the photographs?'

'Lancing in the Homend, I believe.'

'Let us hope that he has not destroyed the plates. We may yet be able to acquire further copies, as you say. After which we will make a thorough search of the fair. If they are hiding Rockstone, I mean to apprehend the fellow.'

* * *

A few minutes later Ravenscroft and Crabb entered the premises of H. Lancing Photographers at the far end of the Homend.

'Thank goodness you have come,' cried out the distressed photographer, coming forwards to meet them.

'Whatever is the matter, Mr Lancing?' asked a concerned Ravenscroft.

'Do please come this way, gentlemen. Something quite terrible has happened.' The photographer led the way into an inner room.

'Good heavens!' exclaimed Crabb.

'All my photographic plates destroyed!' cried out Lancing, pointing to the piles of broken glass and other debris on the floor.

'When did this happen?' enquired Ravenscroft.

'Not ten minutes ago. I returned from an assignment in another part of the town and entered my premises to find this state of destruction. Who can have done such a terrible thing? All my photographic plates destroyed! Totally irreplaceable; images lost to posterity. Who can have done such a thing, Inspector?'

'I am afraid I cannot tell you that Mr Lancing,' sympathised Ravenscroft.

'I sent the boy to fetch you as soon as I discovered what had happened.'

'We did not see him,' said Crabb.

'Then how did you know about this?' asked Lancing.

'We did not. When we returned to the police station this afternoon, we discovered that the photographs you took of the fellow hanged on Hangman Hill had been stolen from our premises.'

'Stolen?' exclaimed Lancing.

'Yes. Your name and details were on the back of the photographs. Whoever took them was also intent on destroying the original plates,' replied Ravenscroft. 'It seems that someone has gone to a great deal of trouble to make sure that no photographic image of the dead man remains. Whoever committed this destruction clearly did not have the time to go through all your plates to find the ones relating to Jacob. I am very sorry, Mr Lancing.'

'Terrible!' The distraught photographer ran his hand through his white hair.

'I will have a word with my superiors and see if we cannot recompense you in some way for your loss. After all, you did produce the photographs upon our instruction. As you said, this must have taken place within the last hour. When you returned, did you see anyone outside the premises, or in the vicinity, acting in a strange way?' asked Ravenscroft.

'No, I believe not, although I do now recall that I did pass by a man on the way down from the railway station. He seemed to be in quite a hurry.'

'Can you describe the fellow to us?'

'Well, he was quite tall, of thin stature, clean-shaven, dark-haired. That is all I can remember.'

'What age do you think he was?'

'Around forty or so, I suppose. He was dressed in a dark overcoat. His hat was pulled down over his face, so that I could not see his features clearly.'

'Do you think that you may have seen this fellow before?'

'No. He was not familiar to me, but as I said, I could not see his face clearly.'

'Thank you, Mr Lancing. I am sorry that you have been caught up in all this trouble.'

'This is all quite upsetting. I only wish I had made further copies,' muttered the photographer, shaking his head, as the two detectives made their way out of the shop.

* * *

'Poor Mr Lancing, and he is such a nice, pleasant man as well,' said Lucy, after she and her husband had each finished narrating their experiences of the day.

'It was just such wanton destruction, but why would the perpetrator of this deed want to prevent any photographic images of poor Jacob surviving?' Ravenscroft poured himself another drink from the decanter.

'So that he could not be identified?' suggested Lucy.

'Exactly, but who really was this man Jacob, and why is someone now anxious to conceal his identity?'

'Perhaps that awful Rockstone is the culprit?'

'I thought so at first, but the description given by Mr Lancing of the man who was hurrying away from his premises does not seem to match Rockstone's appearance.'

'Rockstone could have an accomplice?'

'I suppose that is a possibility, particularly if this accomplice has been providing shelter for Rockstone. Tom and I made a thorough search of the carts and tents of the fairground folk, much to Mr Walker's displeasure, I can tell you — at one stage I thought he was going to assault us — but there was no Mr Rockstone to be found. Until we have discovered the whereabouts of the American, I fear that we will be unable to proceed further with this case.'

'Samuel, I do believe that I might be able to help you,' suggested Lucy tentatively.

'Oh? How is that, my dear?'

'It relates to what Maria Constantine told me this morning. From what she told me about giving away her son, all those years ago, and leaving the locket with the Foundling Hospital, as a kind of token for her son . . . Well, if I were to visit the hospital tomorrow, I might be able to learn more about her son Christopher.'

'I don't think I could let you do that,' protested Ravenscroft.

'Why ever should I not? I am quite capable of travelling up to London on my own. If the hospital could provide me with more information about her son, we might then know whether he was the dead man Jacob or not,' replied Lucy indignantly.

'That would be quite irregular. Anyway I would not like the idea of you travelling alone.'

'Oh do not be so stuffy, Samuel. Nothing is going to happen to me. I would go straight up to London, secure a cab to the Foundling Hospital, find out the information we need, and then return home by the afternoon train. I will be back before you will know that I have gone. Susan can look after little Arthur for the day,' pleaded Lucy.

'The authorities there might not be forthcoming with the information.'

'Why? Is it because I am a woman?'

'No, that is not the reason. It is because you are not a member of the police force, and they would be reluctant to part with the information about this child Christopher.'

'But you could send them a telegram, explaining why you are unable to come in person, requesting them to answer my questions. Oh please say yes, Samuel. If you had seen how that poor woman was so distressed, you would want to do everything in your power to assist her,' pleaded Lucy.

'It was such a long time ago, and I fear that if this Jacob was her son, then it could prove even more upsetting for her. Sometimes the truth can be very painful to accept, and in certain situations it is kinder never to know what has really happened.'

'I cannot believe that you have just said that!' exclaimed Lucy. 'As a detective you have always sought out the truth, and I know you never rest until you have drawn your latest investigation to a satisfactory close. I owe it to Maria Constantine to find out what happened to her son, and I am afraid if you will not give me your blessing to go to London tomorrow, then I shall just have to go without it.'

'I can see that you are quite determined to help Miss Constantine.'

'I am.'

'Then I think you should go. But only on one condition.'

'Yes, yes, anything,' replied Lucy eagerly.

'The condition is that you take the greatest of care, and no matter what you discover at the Foundling Hospital, you are to return home straight away so that we may discuss it together before deciding how to proceed further.' Ravenscroft smiled at his wife's enthusiasm, and her hands in his.

'Of course, Samuel. I would not do anything otherwise.'

CHAPTER FIVE

LONDON

'A fine day, I think you would agree?'

Lucy looked up from her book at the speaker — an American, from his accent.

'I am so sorry. I did not wish to disturb you. Please excuse me, madam.'

Lucy gave a brief smile at the tall, middle-aged gentleman who sat opposite her in the carriage, and then resumed her reading.

When she had joined the London-bound train at Ledbury Station an hour previously, the compartment had been nearly full, her travelling companions consisting of a middle-aged red-faced countrywoman, a young child accompanied by his governess, a soldier, and an elderly gentleman who had been content to retreat behind his copy of the day's *Times*, and the gentleman who had remarked on the condition of the weather. The countrywoman had departed at Worcester station, the soldier at Pershore, the elderly gentleman at Evesham, and the governess and her charge had now left the train at Moreton-in-Marsh.

'I always find this journey interesting, so beautiful the run over the Cotswolds,' said the man, after a few minutes' silence had elapsed. 'Do you travel this way very often?'

'Very rarely,' replied Lucy.

'Once the train has left Reading, the journey presents little of value,' he continued. 'I suppose you are travelling all the way to London?'

'Yes,' said Lucy, feeling uneasy by the other's presence, and hoping that the questions would cease.

'I, too, am travelling to the great metropolis. Although I hail originally from New Hampshire, I have lived over here in your delightful country for the past five years. Much as I like your countryside, and the quaint country towns of Herefordshire, it is always a relief to return to the pleasures of the capital. No offence to Ledbury, of course, which is a delightful place, but I should have no wish to become an inhabitant of the town.'

'It is pleasant enough,' said Lucy formally, trusting that her offhand manner might deter the stranger from continuing further with the conversation.

'You have evidently lived there a long time?'

'About six or seven years,' replied Lucy, realising that perhaps she had said too much.

'I always believe that you can get the feel of a place, and know whether one will be content there, within three hours of one's arrival. I knew when I arrived in London that it was the place for me.'

Lucy said nothing as she looked out of the window of the carriage. As the green fields and small villages passed by, she began to wonder whether this stranger, who spoke in the same manner as Rockstone, and who had joined the train at Ledbury, might even have been an associate of the missing man. She began to wonder whether this stranger has been telling her the truth. She hoped that the train would stop shortly and that they might be joined by other passengers.

He coughed, before producing a small black book from his coat pocket, which he appeared to be reading intently, much to Lucy's relief. A few minutes later the train pulled into the busy station at Oxford, and Lucy was relieved to see a young couple entering their compartment.

Just over an hour later the train drew into Paddington station, and Lucy alighted from the carriage. As she walked along the busy platform, thronged with numerous people all seemingly anxious to begin their business for the day in the great metropolis, she became aware that the American was walking close behind her.

Reaching the cab rank at the back of the station, she joined the line of arrivals.

'Rather a long line, I fear,' smiled the American, standing at her side. 'Perhaps we will do much better if we share a cab. May I ask where you are going to, my good lady?'

'That, sir, is no business of yours. I have no desire to share a cab,' replied Lucy firmly.

'I am sorry, madam. I did not wish to cause any offence.'

Lucy said nothing, as she anxiously sought to attract the attention of one of cabmen.

As the queue gradually edged forwards, Lucy turned, and was pleased to see that the stranger was nowhere to be seen.

'Where would you like to go, madam?' enquired a cheery cabman.

'Russell Square, if you please, and then on to the Foundling Hospital.'

'Right you are. Have you there in fifteen minutes.'

* * *

Lucy alighted from the cab, and after paying the man his due, looked across to the fine, elegant Georgian house, with its two extensions protruding outwards on either side. Although she observed that a number of trees stood in the near vicinity, and that a group of young girls, each wearing a uniform with a white pinafore and cap, were engaged in playing a game of leap-frog on the grass, such an idyllic scene was somewhat spoiled by the thick black smoke that drifted over the whole area.

Lucy walked the few steps to the front door. She turned before reaching for the bell-pull, almost expecting to see again the stranger from the train, but was relieved to find that no one of his description was in the locality.

'Can I be of assistance to you ma'am?' asked a girl of about fifteen, giving a curtsy before her.

'I am Mrs Ravenscroft. I have an appointment to see the Guardian of the Foundling Hospital,' said Lucy, smiling.

'That will be Doctor March; if you would care to come and follow me this way ma'am?'

Lucy entered the building, and followed the girl up a long winding staircase, the walls of which were adorned with fine eighteenth-century portraits.

The girl tapped on a door to the left of the top of the stairs.

'Enter!' called out a voice from within.

'Mrs Ravenscroft to see you, sir,' announced the girl, showing Lucy in.

'Ah, Mrs Ravenscroft, do please come in,' said an elderly grey-haired gentleman rising from his desk and crossing over to the door. 'Thank you, Mary, you may go.'

'Yes, sir.' The girl closed the door behind her.

'Mary is such a pleasant girl; one of our foundlings, of course, and one of our greatest successes. She will shortly be leaving us. I believe she will do well in her new situation,' said March. 'Do please take a seat Mrs Ravenscroft.'

'Thank you,' replied Lucy looking around the fine room with its ornate cornices, bookcases and portraits, before accepting the chair.

'Now then, Mrs Ravenscroft, I am in receipt of your husband's telegram, received earlier this morning,' said March sitting down at the other side of the desk, and peering at the form through a pair of heavy spectacles. 'But I have to tell you that the request asked here is most irregular, most irregular indeed.'

'Oh, why is that, sir?' asked Lucy, feeling somewhat overawed by both the impressive room and its occupant.

'Your husband says here that he is unable to come in person, as he is detained on urgent police business, and that he has sent you in his place, as you are involved in the case,' continued March in a dry formal tone of voice.

'That is so.'

'You gave up a child to the Foundling Hospital?' asked March peering over the top of his spectacles.

'Oh no, I am acting on behalf of another lady.'

'I see. Well I do not think that the foundation can be of any help to you. When our mothers leave their children in our care they do so with the assurance that both the identity of the child and its mother will remain strictly confidential. I am sorry that you have had a wasted journey,' said the doctor, closing the telegram and tossing it on to the desk.

'I am afraid you do not quite understand the reason for my visit,' protested Lucy.

'Then perhaps you should enlighten me Mrs Ravenscroft?'

'The matter is of serious concern. A few weeks ago a man was found dead on one of the hills, near where my husband and I live. He had been killed in a most brutal manner. My husband was unable to identify this man, but was able to recover this item from his effects.' Lucy produced the locket from her handbag, and placed it on the desk in front of March.

'I see.' The doctor picked up the locket and examined it.

'If you will open the locket, you will observe a portrait of a lady inside.'

'A striking image.'

'My husband, Inspector Ravenscroft, was able to identify the artist, and upon visiting him was also able to ascertain the name of the lady depicted there.'

'Go on?' asked March beginning to show an interest.

'He found the lady in question. Many years ago she committed a serious indiscretion, a child was born, but finding herself unable to take her child home she entrusted it to the care of your hospital.'

'I see.'

'The lady left the locket with the child.'

'Ah yes, that is what a great many of our mothers have done in the past. They left a token with the hospital, so that if their personal circumstances changed in the future they could return to reclaim the child.'

'And do many of the mothers do that?'

'I am afraid that only a small number are able to do so. When a child is admitted here we give them a new identity and name, so that they may also be given a fresh start in life. Although this is all very interesting, I still do not see how I can assist you, Mrs Ravenscroft. Why has not the woman in question come forward to take back her child?'

'All of this happened a long time ago; nearly thirty years ago, in fact.'

'I see.'

'The lady could never have taken back her child because of the difficulty of her situation, but now that she has seen the locket she is most anxious to know what happened to him, especially given the circumstances in which the locket was found. My husband is also most concerned to establish the identity of the dead man. Without that information he feels that he may never be able to bring his murderers to justice.' Lucy leaned forward as she sought to press home her case.

'Yes. I can see all of this, but it is still most irregular. It is all a question of confidentiality, you must understand.'

'I appreciate what you are saying. But the child must have left the hospital many years ago, and the lady has given me permission to act on her behalf. If you knew this lady, Doctor March, you would have witnessed the pain this case has caused her. She does not know if her child is still alive, or if he was the murdered man. You are the only person who can be of help. You must have records of what happened to the children?' pleaded Lucy.

'Yes, we do have records.'

'Then I implore you, sir, to assist both the police and this lady in this case.'

March said nothing as he leaned back in his chair, and looked up at the ceiling, deep in thought. Lucy recovered the locket from the top of the desk and placed it in her handbag, knowing that she could do no more.

'As this took place many years ago, as you said, it would do no harm, I suppose, to see what we can find out about this child, but only on the strict assurance that nothing of what you learn today will ever enter the public domain.'

Lucy nodded her head in agreement.

'When was the child admitted?' asked March, rising from his chair.

'In 1862 or early 1863, I believe.'

March walked over to one of the bookshelves, took down two large ledgers and placed them on the desk. 'These are the billet records that were compiled when a child was admitted. I think we will start with this volume. Your search may be very difficult, for we never record either the name of the mother or her baby in the records. The only way in which a mother could later reclaim her child back would be to describe the token that she had left behind originally with the child. The column here gives descriptions of the tokens left, which were then attached to the child's billet, and this records the date of admission and the new name the child was given. Now, let us see.'

For the next few minutes Lucy looked down at the pages in the ledger as March turned over the sheets. Her heart was beating loudly with anticipation that their search might yet prove fruitful.

'Ah, I think we may have found what you are looking for!' exclaimed March suddenly.

Lucy moved closer to the page in question.

'See there — 21 November 1862. Silver Locket containing portrait entitled Maria.'

'That must be the one,' said an excited Lucy.

'Indeed so. The child was given the name Thomas Temple.'

'Not Jacob?' asked Lucy, somewhat disappointed.

'No, Thomas Temple. Our founder was Thomas Coram, and many of the boys were given the Christian name Thomas in memory of the great man. In regard to surnames, a child could be named after a prominent person of the day. Henry John Temple was the British Prime Minister in 1862; you may remember him better by his title of 3rd Viscount Palmerston. The child certainly received a name to be proud of. But I can see, Mrs Ravenscroft, that you were hoping for another name to appear in the register. However once a child obtained maturity, there would be nothing stopping him or her from changing their name to something more to their liking.'

'I understand. Is there any way we can tell what happened to the child?' asked Lucy.

'Yes, indeed. When a child reaches the age of fifteen, he or she must leave the hospital. The girls are often found employment as maids, or in other areas of domestic service. Mary, the girl who you saw earlier, will shortly be leaving us to take up a position in the household of one of our governors. The boys often join the army or navy as cadets, or are apprenticed to professional people, such as a baker's, merchant's, tailor's and so on. We endeavour to match the child's aptitude in each case. We have records of the governors' meetings when such decisions were made, together with copies of the apprentice indentures.'

'This is all most impressive, and to your credit,' remarked Lucy.

'Now, let me see. If young Thomas was admitted in 1862, then he would have been ready to leave us in 1877. I myself was not appointed a governor here until two years later, so obviously I cannot provide you with any recollection of the case,' said March closing the billet book and replacing it on the shelf, before running his fingers along another line of ledgers. 'Ah, here we are. 1877.'

He placed the ledger on the desk and began to thumb through the pages.

'Yes, here we are,' he announced, after a few minutes had elapsed. "Meeting of the Governors, November 1877,

Thomas Temple having attained the age of fifteen, is to be apprenticed as a junior clerk, to Mincing and Stricket, merchants and seedsmen of Limehouse, London." Young Thomas must have done well with his writing and arithmetic to be accorded such an opportunity in life.'

'So Thomas would have left the hospital then, in 1877?'

'Indeed. I can see no further mention of what might have happened to him after that, although I believe the hospital governors would have made a note in any of their further meetings had there been anything contrary to report.' March turned the pages.

'In what way?' enquired Lucy.

'Well, if Mincing and Stricket had gone into insolvency, or if there was evidence that the apprentice had been ill used, if he had absconded, or if he had died, then there would be a record of the event, but looking through these pages I can see no such evidence. I think we can conclude, therefore, that everything went well with young Thomas. And I am afraid that is all I can tell you, Mrs Ravenscroft.'

'Thank you, Doctor March. You have been of great assistance to both my husband and me. I wonder if you have any photographs of the young Thomas?'

'I am afraid not.'

'Well, all the same, Thomas's mother will be pleased with what we have uncovered.'

'Indeed. May I ask what you will do now, Mrs Ravenscroft?' asked March.

'Do you have a copy of the London Street Directory?'

'Indeed,' said March, opening the drawer of his desk, and taking out a large red volume. 'Now how can I help you?'

'Would you be so kind as to see whether Mincing and Stricket are still to be found in Limehouse?'

* * *

'You would do well not to stay too long in this neighbourhood,' remarked the cabman as Lucy alighted in Limehouse.

'There are some rather nasty individuals to be found loitering around the canal entrance down there. Want me to wait for you?'

'No, thank you. I don't quite know how long I will be,' replied Lucy.

'You should find what you are looking for down this road,' called out the cabman as he departed.

Lucy looked around her at the tall buildings and warehouses that crowded in upon one another along the narrow street. Further in the distance she could see a row of old wooden houses, of several storeys in construction, which had clearly seen better days. To her left, in between two of the warehouses, the river was lapping against the sides of the quay, as two or three dogs searched amongst piles of rubbish. A group of ragged children who had been playing near one of the buildings gave Lucy cold stares and disappeared rapidly down one of the nearby alleyways before she could engage them in conversation.

So this was where young Thomas Temple had come in 1877. He must have found this world so different from the close confines of the Foundling Hospital where he was raised for the first fifteen years of his life. Lucy wondered whether he might still be working and living in the area, in which case her search would shortly be over, or whether he had moved on to a better world.

'Lady is lost?'

Lucy turned round to see a Chinese girl of seven or eight looking up at her.

'Yes. I am looking for Mincing and Stricket,' replied Lucy.

'Down there.' The girl pointed at a narrow alleyway running off the street.

'Thank you.' Lucy handed a penny to the child.

The girl grasped the coin, gave a brief smile, and then ran off.

Lucy made her way down the alleyway, looking at the entrances to the buildings on either side as she passed by, until she reached an old brick-built building that had a faded brass plate on its front door bearing the words 'Mincing and Stricket. Merchants.'

Pushing open the door and cautiously entering the building, she found herself standing in a drab, darkened hallway. A grey-haired man was writing in a ledger on a desk at the end of the far end.

'Good morning. Do I have the honour of addressing either Mr Mincing or Mr Stricket?' asked Lucy, edging closer to him as her eyes slowly adjusted to the dim light.

The man went on writing, muttering to himself as he did so.

'Good morning. Mr Mincing?' repeated Lucy in a louder voice.

'Yes?' He looked up from his labour, peering at Lucy over the top of his glasses.

'My name is Mrs Ravenscroft.'

'What? I can't hear you.' He brought a hand up to his ear.

'Mrs Ravenscroft,' said Lucy in an even louder voice.

'Can't hear you. Stricket! Where are you?'

An even older man shuffled into the room.

'Can't hear the lady,' muttered Mincing, resuming his writing.

'Mr Mincing is rather hard of hearing,' said Mr Stricket. 'How may I help you? It is not often we see such a lady as yourself in this area.'

'My name is Mrs Ravenscroft. I presume you are Mr Stricket?'

'I am indeed.'

'I am making enquiries about one of your employees.'

'Oh?' Stricket drew himself up and adopted a more defensive manner.

'The person I am interested in learning more about is a Mr Thomas Temple. I don't suppose he is still with you?' asked Lucy hopefully.

'Lady is asking about a Thomas Tinkle,' shouted Stricket.

'Never heard of him,' replied Mincing, without looking up from his ledger.

'Thomas Temple,' corrected Lucy.

'Thomas who?' enquired Stricket.

'Thomas Temple,' shouted Lucy, now realising that Stricket was probably as deaf as his partner.

'Thomas Temple?'

'He came from the Foundling Hospital, in 1877,' said Lucy, emphasising her words.

'Ah yes, Thomas Temple. I remember Temple,' said Stricket. 'Do you remember young Thomas Temple, Mr Mincing?'

'Thomas Temple? Why yes, Mr Stricket, I remember young Thomas.'

'I don't suppose he is still employed by you?'

'What?' shouted Mincing.

'She wants to know whether young Temple is still with us.'

'Oh, he left us many years ago,' replied Mincing, shaking his head.

'Oh dear, I was rather hoping to speak with him. How long was he with you?'

'How long was young Temple with us, Mr Mincing?' asked Stricket.

'What? Speak up, Mr Stricket.'

'How long was young Temple with us?'

'Four years, I believe. We found him very diligent and industrious.'

'So he left in 1881?' suggested Lucy.' Could you tell me where he went to when he left your employment?

'No, he didn't leave the company. He went to America.'

'To America!'

'Yes, our agent in New York, Mr Forester, died unexpectedly, and needed to be replaced, so we sent young Mr Temple there to take his place.'

'What is that you said Mr Stricket? Forester is dead?' asked a perplexed Mincing.

'Yes, he died in that brawl in the inn. You must remember?'

'Forester dead, you say? Dear me, poor Forester. We will have to send someone to replace him.' Mincing shook his head. 'Dear me, this is most unfortunate.'

'So Thomas Temple went to New York as your agent?' asked Lucy anxious to obtain more information before both partners forgot it. 'What happened to him there? Is he still in New York?'

'We don't know. He worked for us for a year, or eighteen months, and then we heard nothing else from him,' answered Stricket shaking his head.

'Temple? We have not heard from him in a while,' muttered Mincing.

'So Mr Temple went to New York in 1881 as your agent, and worked there for eighteen months,' repeated Lucy.

'That is so,' said Stricket.

'Have you heard anything from him at all during the past ten years?' asked Lucy.

'Nothing at all, I am afraid.' Stricket forced a brief smile.

'Did he leave a forwarding address?'

'Not as far as I know.'

'And you don't know why he left?'

'No. We wrote, of course, but all his letters were returned, and then not at all. We can only suppose that Mr Temple obtained better employment elsewhere.'

'He could have died,' interjected Mincing, much to Lucy's surprise.

'It was all very upsetting at the time. Most unfortunate; he was such a pleasant young fellow,' added Stricket.

'Do you have any photographs by any chance, of Mr Temple?'

'No photographs,' answered Stricket.

'What was that?' asked Mincing.

'Lady was asking if we had any photographs of young Mr Temple,' shouted Stricket.

'Oh no, we never took any photographs.'

'I don't suppose you have Mr Temple's address when he was in New York?' asked Lucy, without any conviction that her question would yield any positive result.

'He boarded at Ma Scrivens' Lodging House in Manhattan,' answered Stricket. 'I remember the name because it was so unusual.'

'So that was where Thomas Temple was living at the time of his disappearance?' asked Lucy.

'Indeed so.'

'Did you write to the lodging house to enquire about Mr Temple's whereabouts?'

'Oh yes, but they never replied.'

'Well thank you both, Mr Stricket and Mr Mincing, you have been most helpful,' said Lucy.

'We do hope you will find Mr Temple, Mrs Raven. He was such a pleasant young man. We have often wondered what had happened to him,' smiled Stricket.

'Who did she say she was?' asked Mincing.

Lucy did not hear Stricket's reply as she made her way out through the door.

* * *

As Lucy began to retrace her steps along the narrow alleyway, she suddenly felt a fierce tugging at her coat.

'Lady help?'

She looked down to see that the speaker was the young Chinese girl whom she had encountered prior to her visit to Mincing and Stricket.

'Please, you help,' said the girl, her eyes full of tears as she looked into Lucy's face.

'Whatever is the matter, my dear?'

'Mother, she sick. You must help,' implored the child.

'What is wrong with your mother?' asked a concerned Lucy.

'Mother have accident,' replied the child tugging harder at Lucy's coat. 'You come. Yes?'

'Well, I don't really know that I should.'

'Mother she is very sick. She die.' The child tugged Lucy towards an open door. 'Mother is in there, on floor.'

Lucy strained to peer through the doorway, and could just glimpse a figure lying on the floor inside the building.

'You help?' implored the girl once more, as the figure gave out a pitiful groan.

'Of course.' Lucy stepped into the room and walked quickly towards the injured woman.

Suddenly the door slammed shut behind her.

Lucy turned round and found herself surrounded by a group of men. The woman on the floor let out a loud laugh as she jumped to her feet. There was no sign of the girl who had enticed her into the room.

'Do not be afraid,' said one of the men.

Lucy dashed towards the door, her way was barred by two rough-looking East End men.

'I demand you get out of my way,' she protested.

'Missie cannot escape,' laughed the man who had spoken first.

'What do you want with me?' asked a frightened Lucy, cursing herself for her own stupidity in entering the room.

'The woman must have something valuable on her,' muttered another of the men.

'Look, I don't know what you want, but I have to tell you that my husband is a police inspector, and that he will stop at nothing until he has found me,' protested Lucy, feeling very afraid as her words were met by laughter from the group.

'Woman, she worth many pounds,' said the woman who had been lying on the floor.

'Nice coat,' said one of the men fingering the fabric.

'Get away from me,' shouted Lucy pushing him away.

'Englishwoman can be exchanged for a lot of opium,' laughed the first man.

'Look, I will give you all I have in my purse,' implored Lucy, as the group of men closed in on her.

'You're a mighty fine woman,' grinned one of the men, displaying a set of badly broken teeth.

'Yeah, women go for a good price,' said another, grabbing Lucy by the arm.

'Let go of me,' shouted Lucy, as yet more of the men began to pull at her coat.

'You're a nice woman,' laughed one of the men.

Suddenly the door crashed open, followed by a loud gunshot.

Lucy screamed as the men loosened their grip on her and scattered to all sides of the room.

'Quickly, follow me!' shouted the new arrival, grabbing Lucy's arm and pulling her towards the door.

As Lucy burst out the room and into the daylight, she recognised her saviour as the American who had spoken to her on the train.

'Follow me, as fast as you can, Mrs Ravenscroft. I have a cab waiting for us round the corner,' said the man waving his gun in the air. 'Those men are dangerous, and it will be all up with both of us if they catch us.'

Lucy ran faster than she had ever done in her life before, as she and the American raced up the alley and round the corner into the street. As she neared a waiting horse-drawn cab, she could hear the sound of distant yells behind her, but feared to look behind less her attackers had closed in upon them.

'Get into the cab!' yelled the American throwing open the door. 'Paddington Station as fast as you can, and lose those ruffians!' instructed the American, following Lucy into the vehicle.

Lucy fought to regain her breath, fearing that her assailants would burst in upon them at any moment. The American flung open the window of the cab, and discharged another shot.

'Don't you worry, Mrs Ravenscroft, they won't trouble us no more.' Her companion closed the window of the cab and replaced the gun in his pocket. 'My, you English people, always getting yourselves in trouble.'

'I cannot thank you enough.' She tried to control her shaking hands.

'Think nothing of it. You should not have travelled into this area. Limehouse is worse than Whitechapel, so they say; full of opium dens and houses of ill repute.'

'How do you know my name?' asked Lucy. 'Do you know my husband?'

'I know of him, but we have never met.'

'What would have happened to me?'

'Oh they would have sold you to one of the brothels, to feed their opium habit, I have no doubt.'

Lucy covered her face with her hands as she felt tears beginning to form in her eyes.

'Here, lady, now don't you go upsetting yourself.' The American handed her a large spotted handkerchief.

'You must think me silly,' said Lucy dabbing her eyes. 'How did you know I was there? Were you following me?'

'Good job I was, lady,' laughed the American.

'Do you know something about Jacob?'

The American banged on the side of the cab. 'Stop here, my man. Take this lady as fast as you can to Paddington Station.' He handed the cabman a coin as he stepped down on to the road.

'But wait, what is your name?' protested Lucy.

'My name is immaterial. Go home, Mrs Ravenscroft. You have had a lucky escape. London is no place for a woman on her own. Give your husband a message from me. Tell him that he would be well advised to give up the case. Nothing good will come of it.'

'But I must—'

'Drive on,' instructed the American, banging on the side of the cab, before disappearing from view.

Lucy sat back in the cab, looked down at her still shaking hands, and found herself living again the terror of the enclosed room.

CHAPTER SIX

LEDBURY

'Well, my dear, I think you have had a very lucky escape,' said Ravenscroft later that evening, after he had listened intently to his wife's adventures in London.

'I was certainly greatly relieved when that American came to my aid. I suppose you are going to reprimand me for going to Limehouse on my own,' said Lucy.

'You did promise that you would come back straight away, after you had been to the Foundling Hospital,' chided Ravenscroft.

'Yes I know, but once I had learned that young Thomas Temple had left the hospital and gone to Mincing and Stricket, then it seemed only sensible that I should go there, and find out what had happened to him. I did not know that those awful people were going to lure me into that room,' said Lucy, trying to appease her husband.

'I am only too pleased that no harm came to you. I do not know what the boys and I would have done without you,' said the detective, taking his wife's hand and pressing it to his lips.

'What I can't understand is what that American was doing following me to Limehouse.'

'He is certainly of interest. You say he was already on the train when you got into the compartment here at Ledbury?'

'Yes. The odd thing is that he knew my name, and yet I am sure I had never met him before, and I certainly never mentioned who I was. He wanted to share a cab with me when we arrived at Paddington, which of course I declined. He was obviously following me, but why?' asked Lucy.

'He must have an interest in this case, and wanted to see where you were going to, and what information you might have obtained about Maria Constantine's son. What did he say when he left you in the carriage?'

'"Tell your husband that he would be well advised to give up the case, and that nothing good will come of it,"' replied Lucy, quoting again the American's words.

'What a strange thing to say. Why would I be well advised to give up the case? It almost sounds like a kind of threat to me, but what was he hiding? Do you know, from the description you have given me, I would say that he very much resembles the man that Mr Lancing saw walking away from his shop, just before he discovered that someone had broken in and destroyed all his photographic plates.'

'The same man who took your photographs of Jacob?'

'Yes, and he made sure that the original photographic plates were also destroyed. I wonder what it is about Jacob that this American did not want us to know. At present we still don't know whether Maria Constantine's son, Thomas Temple, was Jacob. If they were both the same man, then that would perhaps explain the American's interest in following you.'

'Is he connected to Mr Rockstone, I wonder. It is not every day that we have two Americans in Ledbury.'

'Indeed. So, let us see what we have. Maria Constantine gives birth to her son in 1862 but gives him up to the Foundling Hospital in London, in the hope that he could have a better life. In 1877, at the age of fifteen, he is deemed to be of age to make his way in the world, and the hospital authorities apprentice him as a clerk to Mincing and Stricket in Limehouse. Young Thomas obviously does well there, because four years later, when their agent in New York dies in some drunken affray, they decide to send Thomas overseas as their representative. All is well for a year or so, until one day they hear nothing more from Thomas Temple.

'I wonder why? Did he die, or did he seek better employment elsewhere? Then, ten years later, Jacob meets up with Rockstone in New York, and they both come over to England, where they join the fair. Now if Thomas Temple did change his name to Jacob, the question is why did he do that, and also what happened to him between 1882 and now? In my experience people only change their name because they are running away from something, or someone, and are anxious to put the past behind them and start anew.'

'They could still be two different people?' suggested Lucy.

'You could be right. We know that Jacob was afraid when he heard the fair was coming to Hereford, so he must have had some kind of unpleasant experience years ago in the county. Thomas Temple, on the other hand, seems to have gone straight from the Foundling Hospital to Limehouse and then to America. He had no connection with this area, as far as we know. Although his mother came from near here, he was not to know that. Maybe he left New York ten years ago, came to Hereford, became involved in something unpleasant, and then went back to New York.' He made a noise of frustration. 'We are just going round and round in circles all the time. All this is mere speculation.'

'I suppose there have been no sightings of Rockstone?'

'None at all. He seems to have gone completely to ground.' Ravenscroft poured himself another large drink from the decanter.

'Ma Scrivens' Lodging House, Manhattan!' exclaimed Lucy, after a few moments of silence had elapsed. 'That was where young Thomas Temple was lodging when he was working for Mincing and Stricket in New York. That is where you should pick up the trail.'

'You are surely not suggesting that I should travel all the way to New York in the hope that I may be able to find out what happened to Thomas?' said Ravenscroft, somewhat taken aback.

'Why ever not? If that is the only way you can solve this case, then that is what you should do,' said Lucy firmly.

'That is ridiculous!'

'It is not ridiculous at all. Why should you not go?'

'Well, for a start, New York is a big city, full of many thousands of people. It would be like searching for a needle in a haystack. The lodging house may no longer be in existence, and even if I did manage to locate it, I am sure that young Temple would have left there long ago, and then what would I do?'

'Well, you would ask around and find out what had happened to him, like you usually do.'

'No, no, this is quite impossible,' protested Ravenscroft.

'You — we — owe it to Maria Constantine. I am sure you would want to reunite her with her son, if there is any chance that he is still alive,' pleaded Lucy.

'The superintendent would never countenance my sailing off to New York.'

'You don't know until you ask him. If it is the only way this case can be solved, then you should go.'

'But I could not leave you and the children on your own,' pleaded Ravenscroft.

'Why cannot you do that? We can take care of ourselves. I promise I will not be going back to Limehouse ever again! I am sure you would not be away for very long.'

'New York is the other side of the world.'

'There are ships that go from Liverpool.'

'I could not leave the investigation here.'

'Tom is more than capable of taking charge of the search for Rockstone.'

'Yes, I suppose you are right on that count.'

'Then you have no more excuses not to go' said Lucy, with a degree of triumph in her voice.

'I'll give it some thought,' mumbled Ravenscroft.

'In the meantime, I think I should write to Miss Constantine, and tell her what I have discovered about her son.'

'I don't think you should get her hopes up,' said Ravenscroft.

'It is the least I can do. I promised we would help her. Samuel, you must go to New York. You must see that it is the only hope you have of solving this case.'

'We will see what the superintendent has to say about it.'

* * *

'Come in!' boomed a familiar voice from the other side of the door.

Ravenscroft coughed before entering the room.

A large overdressed figure, sporting a red carnation, waved a hand in the direction of a chair placed before the desk. Ravenscroft advanced hesitantly, before sitting down and looking around the drab room with its book-lined shelves and faded photographs.

'Be with you in a minute, Ravenscroft; just fixing this little beauty into position,' said the superintendent, head bent downwards, eyes focused closely on the open glass case before him. 'There we are: the Silver Studded Blue Butterfly. A beauty. Been after her for years. You collect butterflies, Ravenscroft?'

'No, sir.'

'You should do. Rewarding hobby; gives one an interest outside the force. Teaches one all about the world, as well as relaxing the mind.' His superior closed the lid of the case.

'I'm afraid I have never had the time, nor the inclination,' replied Ravenscroft.

'Damn poor show I call that,' muttered his superior giving him a look of disapproval. 'Well what can I do for you, Ravenscroft?'

'It's the murder in the hills, sir — the hanging.'

'Yes, been reading your report,' said the superintendent, tapping a folder on his desk. 'Not making much progress, are we?'

'I am afraid not.'

'Still haven't caught this Rockstain fellow.'

'Rockstone, sir,' corrected Ravenscroft.

'Yes, yes, Rockstain, Rockstone, whatever his name. We can't have these Americans causing havoc over here and then disappearing.'

'I can assure you that we are doing our best to apprehend him.'

'Got to find him first,' said the superintendent sarcastically.

'Yes, sir.'

'Now you want to go off halfway round the world to New York, of all places. Well I'm afraid it just won't do. It won't do at all. It is totally out of the question.'

'It may be the only way we can solve this murder, sir. If I can discover the whereabouts of this Thomas Temple in New York, I may be able to find out who hanged Jacob,' said Ravenscroft, realising that he was probably not going to succeed with his request.

'The word is "may", as you say.'

'If I don't try, I fear this will go down in our archives as an unsolved case.'

'Don't like unsolved crimes; bad for morale.'

'Precisely, sir.'

'No, no. It just won't do. Sending one of my officers to the other side of the world on some wild goose chase? We haven't got the money. And if you go, who is going to run things in Ledbury and continue the search for this Rockstone person?'

'Constable Crabb is very able. He has been with me for over four years now, and during all that time I have found him most industrious and diligent.'

'Yes, yes,' replied Ravenscroft's superior, showing signs of irritation. 'No, it just won't do. We cannot afford the expense, and that's an end to the matter.'

'I believe I have some leave due, sir,' said Ravenscroft deciding to change course.

'I suppose you have.'

'Then if I chose to go to New York at my own expense, and in my own time, I trust you would have no objection? Crabb is more than capable of continuing the case over here in my absence.'

'I don't know, Ravenscroft. If it ever got out that I had sent one of my officers all the way to New York, we could be made to look a laughing stock.'

Ravenscroft looked disappointedly down at the floor. 'I would of course be acting entirely on my own; there would be no need to involve the New York police in any way.'

'Sorry, Ravenscroft. I know you have put a great deal of effort into the solving of this case, but I cannot permit such an enterprise. Close the door behind you, won't you?'

'Butterflies!' exclaimed Ravenscroft, an idea coming into his mind.

'Butterflies? What about butterflies?'

'I understand that there are some rather rare butterflies to be found in America?'

'That is correct.'

'Perhaps if I could locate one or two dealers of butter-flies, registered in New York, I could bring back one or two specimens,' suggested Ravenscroft, realising that his request might be about to take a more positive direction.

'Excellent suggestion, Ravenscroft! What a capital idea! You should have mentioned it earlier.'

'Then you would have no further objections if I went, in my own time, as I have just said?'

'Absolutely!' said the superintendent rising from his desk. 'Marvellous, but you must let me contribute towards the cost of your fare. Where are you sailing from?'

'There is a Cunard ship leaving Liverpool the day after tomorrow, the *Etruria*,' replied Ravenscroft. 'I will accept your most generous offer, if I may. I will see what I can bring back with me.'

'That is wonderful news, Ravenscroft. I'll just give you the names of one or two North American butterflies that I am especially keen to acquire. Capital.'

'Oh, and just before I go, sir, I wonder if I might have a word with you about another pressing matter?'

* * *

The following morning found Ravenscroft and Lucy on the platform of Ledbury Station, with Crabb standing discreetly a few feet away.

'Now, my dear, you must promise me that you will not be going off on any more adventures to Limehouse during my absence,' said Ravenscroft.

'I give you my word, Samuel. Do stop worrying. The boys and I will be just fine.' Lucy brushed away a hair from the top of his coat.

'I should be back within two to three weeks. The crossing is usually seven or eight days, and I don't intend staying in New York for longer that I have to.'

'You must remain there as long as you consider necessary. I've packed your case with everything I think you will need. I have taken the liberty of including some reading material for the voyage, should you find yourself becoming bored,' smiled Lucy.

'Sherlock Holmes?' asked Ravenscroft hopefully.

'*Barchester Towers*. Anthony Trollope. It is quite long, but not as long as some of his other novels, and yes, I did find you the latest edition of *The Strand Magazine*, which has another story by Mr Conan Doyle.'

'Excellent.'

'And if you get bored you can always start writing your memoirs.'

'I don't think so.'

'And make sure you wrap up well on that ship, it is bound to be quite cold and windy,' instructed Lucy. 'I have heard that the Atlantic can often be a rough crossing at this time of year.'

'Of course I will. I am going to miss you frightfully. I rather wish I was not going now.'

'Now, Samuel, you know that we must do all that we can to help Miss Constantine. Just make sure that you come back to us. I think I can hear the train approaching.'

'I had better have a word with Tom,' said Ravenscroft walking across towards the constable.

'I wish you well with your travels, sir,' said Crabb.

'You have my full authority to act on your own initiative during my absence. I am sure you will manage quite well. I hope you apprehend Rockstone. If he killed Jacob, I want to know why. I have every faith in you, Tom.'

'Thank you, sir.'

'Oh yes, and make sure we know where the travelling fair is going to during the next two months or so, should we need to question Walker and his associates further,' shouted Ravenscroft above the noise of the steam train as it pulled into the station.

'Yes, sir.'

'Take care, Samuel! Come back safely to us,' cried out Lucy as Ravenscroft hauled his case into the compartment.

'Goodbye, my dear! Goodbye, Tom!' shouted the detective as the train pulled out of the station.

Lucy and Crabb waved, and watched in silence as the train turned the corner and disappeared from view.

'Well, Tom, it looks as though we are on our own now,' said Lucy.

'Indeed so, Mrs Ravenscroft. I am sure it will not be long before the inspector safely returns.'

CHAPTER SEVEN

AT SEA

Ravenscroft flung the book on to the hard and uncomfortable berth and gave out a deep sigh.

The *Etruria* had left Liverpool three days earlier, and although the sea had been relatively calm at the time of its departure, by the end of the next day a violent storm had driven its passengers, Ravenscroft among them, to seek the sanctuary of their cabins.

At first Ravenscroft had almost welcomed the opportunity of retreating to his simply furnished second-class cabin, but having long exhausted the contents of the latest edition of *The Strand Magazine*, and finding that the Proudies and Hardings of Barchester were a people that he could not quite take to, he had begun to tire of the confines of the little room with its continual pitching back and forth and its creaking boards, and longed for a calmer sea and a tranquil voyage so that he might walk about once more.

Lying stretched out on his bed he found his mind turning again to the case in hand. Quite why he had agreed to embark on this adventure to a strange country, he could not be sure. Even if he did locate the lodging house where the young Thomas Temple had boarded over ten years ago, there was still no guarantee that the man would still be there. If Temple had left the residence all those years ago it was doubtful whether anyone would remember him, or know where he had gone to. If Temple had travelled to another part of America, or returned to England, or gone to anywhere else in the world, then the search would prove almost impossible.

If he was fortunate in his quest to find Temple, that at least would prove that he was not the man known as Jacob, and he would then be able to reunite Maria Constantine with her son. But, he reminded himself, if he found Temple perhaps the fellow might not wish to abandon the life he had created for himself in the New World, for the sake of a mother who had abandoned him when he had been only an infant. And for his professional purpose, it might be better if he could establish that Temple had also been Jacob. At least that way he might be able to discover who Jacob was, and why he had been killed. But the hope of solving the murder of the dead man on Hangman Hill now seemed a remote possibility.

No, it had been foolish to even think that this mad adventure could yield anything of value. He should have remained in Ledbury and carried on the search for Rockstone. He was still convinced that it was the travelling quack who held the key to this mystery. He cursed himself for his folly.

A loud knock on his cabin door broke into his deliberations.

'Good evening, sir,' said the cheery steward, opening the door.

'Evening already?' asked Ravenscroft, rising from his bed.

'Six o'clock, sir. You will be pleased to know that the storm has abated.'

'Thank goodness. Does that mean that I can now go up on to the deck? That is good news indeed.'

* * *

A few minutes later, after climbing, with difficulty, up two flights of steps on the *Etruria*, Ravenscroft found himself on the promenade deck of the vessel. Although the steward had claimed that the storm had ended, Ravenscroft was not so sure of that assertion. He clung to the rail at the side of the deck in an attempt to prevent the wind from blowing him elsewhere, and looked out across the huge waves that crashed into the side of the ship. As he attempted to clear his spectacles from the spray that covered the lenses, the detective began to wish that he had remained in the landlocked town of Ledbury, and cursed the folly of his decision to sail across the unpleasant ocean.

'You get used to it after a while.'

Ravenscroft turned to find that he had been joined by a tall, grey-haired, elderly gentleman, dressed in a thick astrakhan overcoat and fur hat.

'I don't think that will ever be the case,' he replied.

'Oh, when you have made the crossing a few times, you kind of get used to all the wind and rain,' continued the man. His accent marked him as an American.

'I only intend making this one crossing and the return journey. I have no inclination to set sail ever again.'

'You say that now, but I can assure you that once the sun is out tomorrow, and the sea is calm, it will seem like a different world out here.'

'You know that tomorrow will be different?' asked Ravenscroft hopefully.

'I believe so, but then again I could be wrong.'

'You make this crossing a great deal?'

'Generally two or three times a year. I try to avoid the winter months. It can be quite cold and icy in New York in January and February.'

'So I believe. I am glad it is October.'

'Can get rather foggy now, but you should not encounter many problems. So this will be your first visit to our fine city?'

'Indeed.'

'I take it your visit is one based on business rather than pleasure?'

'Your assumption is correct.'

'Sorry, we have not been introduced, and I know you English like your formalities. My name is William O'Callaghan. I'm in the export and import business.'

'Samuel Ravenscroft.'

'And what line of business brings you to New York, Mr Ravenscroft?' asked the American.

'Butterflies,' replied Ravenscroft, not wanting to give away his true occupation to the stranger.

'Butterflies!' exclaimed the American. 'Well I never! You English. You are coming all this way for butterflies?'

'Yes, I believe there are some rather rare butterflies in North America. I hope to acquire some specimens for me and my friends, to add to our collections,' answered Ravenscroft, regretting that he had been so forthcoming on a subject of which he knew so little about, and fearing that he might be caught out by the stranger at any moment.

'Well I've heard it all now. I know people collect fine furniture, paintings and other bygone relics, but it's the first time I've ever met anyone who collects butterflies. England is full of eccentrics — that's what I like about the place,' said the American, giving out a hearty laugh.

'You say your name is O'Callaghan?' asked Ravenscroft, quickly seeking to turn the conversation in another direction, but wishing that the loud American would go away.

'My grandfather was Irish. He came from a little village in County Kerry. Then he fell on hard times and took his family off to America to seek a better life — and do you know, he found it there. America really is a land of opportunity. I was born in New York, so I can say that I am a hundred per cent American, and proud of it as well.'

'I am sure you are. May I ask what you export and import?'

'Confidential, my friend,' replied the American defensively, as he stared sternly at Ravenscroft.

'I am sorry, I did not wish to pry,' said Ravenscroft realising that he might have caused some offence with his question.

'I know. You English, always wanting to know what we old colonials are up to,' laughed the American, quickly reverting to his former way of speaking. 'Mr Ravenscroft, I think you and I are going to get on with each other just fine. Why don't you have dinner with me tomorrow evening, and you can tell me more about those quaint old butterflies you are so interested in.'

'I would not wish to intrude—' began Ravenscroft.

'No intrusion, sir, I can assure you.'

'Well, that is most kind of you, Mr O'Callaghan.'

'Good, that is settled, then. See you at seven tomorrow evening, in the first-class dining room?'

'I am afraid I am only travelling second class,' said Ravenscroft, hoping that this excuse would prove sufficient for the invitation to be rescinded.

'No problem. I will have a word with the head waiter. Now if you will excuse me, I think I've had enough of this Atlantic air for one night.'

'Good night, Mr O'Callaghan.'

Ravenscroft watched as the American made his way along the deck and in through one of the doors, wondering what had possessed him to accept a dinner invitation from a man he scarcely knew, and who he did not particularly like.

* * *

The next day the sun did indeed shine, and Ravenscroft took the opportunity of walking up and down the promenade deck of the *Etruria* in the morning, before acquiring one of the deck chairs at the quieter end of the vessel which also afforded some shelter from the wind.

After lunch he visited the ship's library and asked the librarian there whether the collection included any books on butterflies, and was somewhat relieved when the man took down a large volume from one of the shelves. Ravenscroft then retired to a corner of the saloon, where he spent the remainder of the afternoon turning over its pages, and attempting to memorise the names of those butterflies that were known to be resident species of North America.

It was a rather hesitant Ravenscroft who entered the first-class dining room just after seven that evening. As he gave his name to the head waiter at the door, he hoped that even now he would be refused admittance, but it appeared that the waiter knew of his impending arrival and escorted him to a corner of the room, where he found his host already in residence.

'Ah, Mr Ravenscroft, glad you could come. May I introduce you to my two fellow travellers, Mr Petters and Mr Foy,' said the American standing up from the table.

'Good evening, gentlemen,' replied Ravenscroft, observing that whereas the first gentleman was of an overweight and red-faced appearance, his companion was thin, and showed signs of a nervous disposition.

'Come, don't' wait on ceremony.' O'Callaghan indicated that Ravenscroft should occupy the remaining seat.

'Thank you.'

'Mr Ravenscroft here is a collector of butterflies, and would you believe it, he is travelling all the way across to New York in the hope of adding to his collection.'

'Yes, indeed,' replied Ravenscroft somewhat apprehensively.

'I had an uncle who once collected buttons,' said Petters.

'Buttons!' exclaimed O'Callaghan. 'What the heck would anyone want from collecting something as dull as buttons!'

'He didn't think they were dull,' retorted Petters.

'And what do you collect, Mr Foy?' asked Ravenscroft, saying the first thing that came into his head.

Foy said nothing, only stared at Ravenscroft. His left eye twitched as he did so.

'You must excuse our friend Mr Foy. He is a man of few words. Isn't that so, Foy?' said O'Callaghan, touching his friend on the shoulder.

'If you say so,' muttered Foy, with another twitch of his face, before he looked vacantly into the distance.

'Now what would you like, Mr Ravenscroft?' said his host as the waiter handed the detective a large menu.

'Wish this voyage would soon be over,' grumbled Foy, as Ravenscroft studied the menu.

'Mr Foy is not a good traveller, are you, Foy? I think he prefers a horse,' laughed O'Callaghan. 'Now, Mr Ravenscroft, tell us more about these butterflies of yours. I am sure that my colleagues, Mr Petters and Mr Foy, would be most interested to learn more about your great interest.' O'Callaghan looked intently at the detective as a waiter lit a large cigar for him.

'Well . . . I . . . er . . . I have not been collecting them for very long,' replied Ravenscroft, before going on to name a number of butterflies, which he had read in the book he had borrowed earlier from the library, and hoping that he would not be found out by any of his dining companions.

'Seems you know quite a lot about your subject. But where do you put all these dead butterflies?' asked O'Callaghan.

'Oh, I mount them on card, and put them in trays in a cabinet,' replied Ravenscroft remembering his superior's collection back in Worcester.

'And which butterflies do you wish to acquire in New York?' asked O'Callaghan, staring intently at Ravenscroft before puffing on his cigar.

The detective struggled to remember the names of several of the creatures his superior had mentioned to him before leaving England.

'Well, that is pretty impressive, is it not gentlemen?' said O'Callaghan, turning towards his two companions.

'Very,' remarked Petters without enthusiasm, as he poured himself another glass of wine. Foy gave a sigh and twitched once more.

'And where do you hope to acquire these butterflies, Mr Ravenscroft?' asked O'Callaghan.

'I believe there are one or two dealers in butterflies in New York.'

'Well I'll be darned, who would have thought there were dealers in New York selling that kind of thing?' laughed O'Callaghan. 'We shall have to see if we can assist Mr Ravenscroft in his search, will we not, Mr Petters?'

'Indeed,' replied Petters without interest.

* * *

Two hours later, Ravenscroft sought the quiet sanctuary of his cabin. The dinner had been a daunting experience. Mr Petters had been particularly blunt in his answers, almost to the point of rudeness, whereas his companion Foy had said so little during the evening that Ravenscroft had found it difficult to avert his gaze from the man's uncontrollable twitching. But it had been O'Callaghan's continual questioning and accompanying stare that had unsettled him the most. He had done his best not to give away either his true occupation, or the real reason for his visit to New York, while trying to pass himself off as an eccentric English butterfly collector, but as the evening had progressed Ravenscroft had become gradually aware that perhaps his dining companions had begun to see through the facade he had created. Then there had been the large waves of smoke from the American's cigar, which had drifted irritatingly across the table in his direction, the loudness of his host's boisterous conversation, and the particularly aggressive manner in which Petters ate his food, which had all added to the unpleasantness of the evening.

Ravenscroft had formed a great dislike of the three men. He had met Americans before during his long years in Whitechapel, some of whom had been outgoing and untrustworthy in their nature. Some had even been violent; one or two had even been arrested for murder. But these men were different. Something told him that these Americans were not to be trusted, and that any future contact with them was fraught with possible danger.

As Ravenscroft undressed and retired to his bed he resolved to avoid any future contact with the three men for the remainder of the voyage.

* * *

After an unsettled night during which he had dreamt of large swarms of butterflies circling and attacking him in a large field, and had awoken several times in a cold sweat, Ravenscroft climbed out of his bed and made his way across the room to the water jug to relieve his dry throat. As he poured himself some water into a glass he observed that a note had been pushed under the door of his cabin. He bent down, picked up the paper and read its contents.

> *Keep away from O'Callaghan. He is not to be trusted. He is a dangerous man. Believe me when I say that I have your best interests at heart.*
> *A Friend.*

Ravenscroft read the note several times and examined the large untidy hand in which it had been written. Who could possibly have penned such a letter? He had not made the acquaintance of anyone else on the ship, so it seemed unlikely that this so-called 'friend' could have been known to him. It was also unlikely that either of O'Callaghan's companions, Petters or Foy, would have sent the message. Why was he now being warned against O'Callaghan? He certainly did not like the American or his companions, and wished he had never dined with them, but he had to remind himself that although he distrusted them, his dislike of them did not necessarily make them criminals.

Then Ravenscroft remembered the words that Lucy's saviour had uttered when he had left her cab *'tell your husband he would be well advised to give up the case; he would do well to leave things alone.'* He wondered whether this new message could also have been written by the same person. If so, why had this man warned him against following up the Jacob case, as well as now advising him to keep away from O'Callaghan and his companions? Did the three Americans have something to do with Jacob's murder? Perhaps Thomas Temple had also been known to these men?

Ravenscroft knew that he did not have the answers to these questions, but he now realised that there were others on the ship intent on taking a keen personal interest in his activities. He was also conscious that he was about to enter a new country, where he would be very much on his own, where there would be no Crabb or any other police colleagues he would be able to call upon should he be in need of them. He knew now that he would need to be even more diligent than usual, and be on his guard against anything, or anyone, that might prevent him from learning the truth.

* * *

The remainder of the voyage seemed to Ravenscroft to pass quite quickly, and by keeping very much to himself he was able to avoid any further contact with the three Americans.

On the final day of the voyage Ravenscroft made his way out onto the deck. The early morning mist was already beginning to clear, and the gradual appearance of a number of buildings in the distance was a welcoming sight after so many days at sea. He knew it would not be long before he could disembark, and he could make his way to Ma Scrivens' Lodging House, where hopefully he could begin his investigations.

Ravenscroft returned to his cabin as the ship pulled into the harbour side and other passengers began to gather on the decks, as he had no desire to encounter O'Callaghan and his two companions during his departure.

After a few minutes had elapsed Ravenscroft tipped his cabin steward, and carrying his suitcase he made his way down to the gangplank and felt once again the reassuring steadiness of land. He joined the throng of passengers on the quay side, and after completing the required formalities he made his way through a large building and out into the open air, where he observed a line of cabs waiting to take the new arrivals into the city.

'Ravenscroft man, jump up here and I'll give you a lift,' shouted out a familiar voice from the inside of a cab, which drew up suddenly in front of him.

'I think I will be fine, I thank you,' he replied, realising that the speaker was O'Callaghan.

'That's nonsense man; where are you headed?'

'Scrivens' Lodging House,' replied Ravenscroft somewhat hesitantly.

'Fine; I am going the same way. Get in,' replied the American throwing open the door with some force, so that it almost hit Ravenscroft in the face.

'I am sure it is an inconvenience,' stuttered Ravenscroft, hoping that O'Callaghan might yet rescind his invitation, and he could yet avoid any further contact with him.

'Rubbish man. You'll have the devil of a wait over there. Don't stand on ceremony. Get in man.'

Ravenscroft reluctantly stepped into the cab, which he found occupied by O'Callaghan and the man Foy.

'You English, always so darned reticent.'

'That is most kind of you,' replied a somewhat nervous Ravenscroft.

'Staying at Ma Scrivens' then?' asked O'Callaghan.

'Yes, it was recommended to me by a friend.'

'Do you hear that, Foy? Our English friend here says that Ma Scrivens' was recommended to him by a friend,' laughed O'Callaghan.

'Really,' said Foy sourly with a twitch of his face.

'God man you don't want to stay at that dreadful forsaken place. You won't last two days there. Look why don't you stay at my hotel?'

'That is very kind of you, but I feel I must decline. I have already made a reservation,' protested Ravenscroft, a sickening feeling in his stomach.

'Well you can cancel it. You come and stay with us.'

'No, really, I can't.'

'Why ever not man?'

'I am meeting a friend of mine, who is already staying there,' said Ravenscroft, thinking quickly as he could to come up with some excuse.

'Well if you must. What do you think of New York so far?'

'It seems very noisy, and busy,' replied Ravenscroft looking out of the window of the cab.

'Yep, there is sure plenty going on here. We are always on the move; building everywhere. We will soon run out of space, then I guess we will just have to build upwards into the sky.'

Ravenscroft gave a brief smile as he continued to watch the sights of the city as the cab made its way along the busy streets.

'I tell you Ravenscroft, London ain't got nothing on this place.'

'No, I suppose not.'

A few minutes later the cab turned down a narrow road, eventually stopping outside a large five storey building situated at the corner of two streets.

'That's Ma Scrivens'. If you don't like the look of it, my offer still stands,' said O'Callaghan leaning forwards and breathing closely into Ravenscroft's face.

'No, it will be fine,' replied the detective beginning to alight from the cab.

'See here Ravenscroft you just take my card. It has the name of my hotel on it. Feel free to come and join us anytime you like,' urged O'Callaghan thrusting the item into Ravenscroft's hand.

'Thank you for the ride,' said the detective taking the card and closing the cab door behind him.

'Be seeing you!' shouted O'Callaghan as the cab sped off in a cloud of dust.

Ravenscroft let out a deep sigh of relief and looked up at the tall building. For a moment he thought he had stepped backwards in time, for the drab, untidy structure, with its peeling paint, damaged rusty wrought iron balconies and decaying woodwork, reminded him of some of the most notorious slums that he had experienced during his police days in Whitechapel. A board bearing the name 'Scrivens' Lodging House' hung crookedly over the entrance door, and a smell of smoke and decaying rubbish seemed to hang over the whole neighbourhood. Perhaps it had been unwise of Ravenscroft to contemplate staying in such a residence, but he told himself that if he was to discover what had happened to Thomas Temple then then he would have to put any reservations he had about the lodging house to one side, and at least he had managed to escape from the overbearing O'Callaghan and his companion.

Ravenscroft pushed open the door and found that he was now facing a large wooden counter at the end of a passageway, behind which stood an elderly man with a long flowing beard, wearing untidy clothes and lopsided wire spectacles.

'Good morning. I would like a room please,' said Ravenscroft.

'You ain't from round these parts then?' enquired the man without looking up from the book he had been reading.

'England,' replied Ravenscroft placing his case on the floor. 'I've just disembarked from the Etruria.'

'What do you want a room for?' said the man looking up and staring hard at Ravenscroft.

'I was under the impression that this was a lodging house, and anyway I have nowhere else to stay.'

'How long?'

'Pardon?'

'How long do you want to stay for?'

'For two or three days; I am not quite sure at this moment.'

The man stared again intently at Ravenscroft for a few seconds without saying anything, before suddenly calling out 'Ma!'

Ravenscroft shuffled his feet as the man repeated the call, without success.

'Look surely you can give me a room,' protested Ravenscroft finding that the man's inhospitable manner was beginning to annoy him.

The man yelled the same command for a third time.

Suddenly a door to the left of the counter sprang open. 'What do you want?' shouted a tall, red sweaty faced, heavily built woman entering the room.

'Gent here wants a room, Ma. He says his from England. Just got off one of them boats,' said the old man.

'Does he? Why has he come here?' replied the woman in an aggressive tone, addressing her question to the man rather than to Ravenscroft himself.

'Your establishment was recommended to me,' interjected Ravenscroft.

The man gave out a hearty laugh.

'Who by?' asked the woman.

'You were recommended by a friend of mine in England, who once lodged with you here.'

'Did he? That's as may be,' said the woman in a dismissive tone.

'Look, is this house a boarding establishment, or is it not?' asked an irritated Ravenscroft raising his voice.

'It is.'

'So you have rooms? I would be obliged if I can have one of them.'

'Put him in number 5,' replied the woman, before turning her back and exiting quickly through the door.

The clerk opened a large ledger. 'Sign here,' he indicated with a dirty brown withered finger.

Ravenscroft entered his name. 'I presume that was Ma Scriven?' he asked.

'Yep,' replied the clerk, closing the ledger with a bang. 'That will be ten dollars in advance. Dinner is at seven.'

Ravenscroft handed over the money. The man resumed his writing.

'Could you tell me where number 5 is?' asked Ravenscroft after a moments silence had elapsed, during which time he realised that the man did not seem inclined to either show him the way or carry his case for him to his new abode.

'Up the stairs, turn right, up the stairs, turn left, up the stairs, third door on right,' replied the man, after giving out a loud sigh.

'Thank you,' said Ravenscroft picking up his case.

'You need that,' said the man, banging a large key on the counter before turning on his heel and walking out of the side door.

Ravenscroft picked up the key and began to make his way up the first flight of stairs. Pausing only to look at the peeling walls and threadbare carpet on the first landing, he then continued to follow the clerk's instructions and began the ascent of the second narrower flight of stairs. Upon reaching the next landing he rested for a moment to ease his congested lungs, before proceeding upwards onto the third landing, where he located the third door on the right, which bore a faded sign indicating that he had at last reached the end of his journey.

Opening the creaking door, Ravenscroft entered and looked round the simply furnished room, which consisted of a brass bedstead, wooden wardrobe and chair, and side table upon which stood a chipped jug and bowel. A faded coloured print of the Virgin Mary hung crookedly from one of the walls, and he observed that the colour of the bed cover was of a dubious nature.

Placing his case on the floor and removing his coat, Ravenscroft crossed over to the window and strained to peer through the dirt-stained pane. Opposite him was a building of similar structure and height, which appeared to be in no better condition than the house he had just entered, and to either side of it the view extended over crowded streets and houses, stretching forever into the distance. Black clouds of smoke rising from numerous factories drifted across the city, and although it was only midday it seemed more like early evening.

Ravenscroft reached into his coat pocket, took out the locket and gazed at the portrait inside, before casting another glance round the miserable room. He wondered whether this had been the actual room where Temple had lodged upon his arrival in American, and if so, that might have explained why the young man had one day left it all behind him.

Ravenscroft wondered whether he had perhaps been foolish to have left Ledbury and to have undertaken such a long journey halfway around the world on what might well prove to be a futile quest. Would he be able to find out what had happened to Thomas Temple all those years ago? And if he did eventually track down the missing man, would that then enable him to finally discover who had murdered Jacob — or would his investigations lead to nothing?

Feelings of apprehension and despair suddenly seemed to overwhelm Ravenscroft, as he felt the utter loneliness of his present situation. Throwing himself down on the bed with a deep sigh, he looked up at the large damp patch on the ceiling above him and resolved that he would endeavour to make his stay in the metropolis as short as possible.

CHAPTER EIGHT

THE ORCHARDS

Lucy closed the door of the cottage behind her, and walked down the cobbled street to the marketplace in Ledbury.

On the day after her husband's departure for New York she had written a letter to Maria Constantine detailing her experiences in London, and telling her of how her son Thomas had fared at the Foundling Hospital and then at Mincing and Stricket, before his departure for America. She had ended with the news of Ravenscroft's journey to the New World. Earlier that day she had received a reply, in which Maria Constantine had expressed both her gratitude and her hopes for the future. Now Lucy's thoughts turned once more to the event on Hangman Hill.

'Good morning, Tom,' said Lucy, entering the tiny police station in Ledbury.

'Good morning, Mrs Ravenscroft,' replied the young policeman with a smile.

'I was just passing so I thought I would see how the investigation is progressing.'

'Not as well as I would have hoped. In fact we've have no luck at all in catching the elusive Mr Rockstone. He seems to have vanished into thin air. I would not be surprised if he has gone back to America.'

'Never mind,' sympathised Lucy.

'Perhaps Inspector Ravenscroft will have better fortune with his enquiries in New York. He should have arrived by now.'

'Indeed,' answered Lucy. 'I have been thinking much about this case. Don't you think it unusual that Jacob was hanged in such an inaccessible place as Hangman Hill? Don't murderers usually pick somewhere a little easier to lure their victims to?'

'It's not the first time I have asked myself the same question, Mrs Ravenscroft. It does seem rather odd. They could have hanged the poor man from any tree.'

'Yes. It is as though the hill had some significance for whoever committed the crime.'

'As if something terrible happened there, years ago,' suggested Crabb.

'Exactly. Whatever took place there must have happened before either you or I came to the area, or we would have known about it.'

'Those were my thoughts entirely.'

'How can we find out about the hill and what might have happened there?'

'I know just the person who might be able to answer that question,' answered Crabb enthusiastically. 'If I bring the horse and trap, would you care to accompany me to Malvern, Mrs Ravenscroft?'

'Yes indeed.'

* * *

Later that morning Lucy and Crabb made their way along Belle Vue Terrace in Malvern, until they reached the Malvern Library and Reading Rooms at the corner of the road.

'Good morning, madam, and Constable Crabb,' said Clifford the librarian as they entered the building.

'Mr Clifford, may I introduce you to Mrs Ravenscroft,' said Crabb.

'I am delighted to make your acquaintance, Mrs Ravenscroft.'

'I have heard so much about you and your excellent library, Mr Clifford,' smiled Lucy.

'The good inspector is not with you this morning?'

'He is away on business,' replied Lucy not wanting to give too much information away regarding her husband's activities.

'Then how can I be of assistance to you?'

'It is regarding the death of that man on Hangman Hill,' said Crabb.

'Ah, yes.'

'We were wondering whether anything else of a tragic nature has ever occurred on that hill?' asked Lucy.

'Not as far as I am aware. Of course I have only been here in Malvern for the past seven years,' replied Clifford in his usual polite formal manner.

'This event could have happened ten or more years ago,' suggested Crabb.

'We thought that you might have some records that we could examine?' added Lucy.

'If something of a serious nature did occur on the hill, then it would have been recorded in the *Malvern News*. We do have back copies of the newspaper here, but it would take a great deal of time to go through them.'

'Then perhaps we should make a start, Mr Clifford?' said Crabb.

'Of course, if you would both care to follow me into the other room,' said Clifford, leading them to the same inner room, lined with volumes of books and newspapers, that Ravenscroft and Crabb had been in two weeks earlier.

'The newspaper is bound in volumes, and each volume contains approximately three months of weekly issues. Where would you like to start?' asked Clifford.

Lucy and Crabb looked at one another.

'Perhaps I might suggest that you commence with 1880 and work forward until say, 1884? If you do not find anything there, then you can investigate the older copies.'

'That would be most acceptable,' said Lucy, taking the seat that the librarian offered.

Clifford brought over two large volumes, and gave one each to Crabb and Lucy. 'I am afraid I must leave you to your task, as I have one or two other customers I must see to in the lounge. The other volumes are clearly marked on the shelves behind you.'

'Thank you, Mr Clifford,' said Lucy.

'I wish you well with your search,' smiled Clifford as he left the room.

'Well, we had better make a start,' said Lucy opening the large volume.

During the next hour, both Lucy and Crabb turned over the weekly pages of the *Malvern News*, twice replacing the volumes that had been selected by the librarian.

'I think we have it!' exclaimed Lucy.

Crabb stood up and looked over Lucy's shoulder as she read from the volume.

TRAGEDY ON THE HILLS
YOUNG   WOMAN   FOUND   DEAD   ON
HANGMAN HILL

The body of a young woman was recovered last Monday evening from the summit of Hangman Hill on the Malvern Hills.
It is understood that the deceased, Lizzie Warren, was employed as a milkmaid at Orchard Farm, Parkway near Ledbury, Herefordshire, and had been out walking on the hills, when she fell and sustained a fatal injury. The incident was reported to the local constabulary in Malvern, but our reporter has been informed by Inspector Robinson that no foul play is suspected.

'Well it seems that we were right, Mrs Ravenscroft. Something terrible did happen on that hill, all those years ago' said Crabb.

'The poor thing. How unfortunate. Tom, do you think we can find out anything else about this case?' asked Lucy.

'There could be a police file. I will make enquiries.'

'I wonder if there were any further reports in the newspaper?' said Lucy turning over the pages. 'Yes, here we are. There are just a few lines giving news of the inquest. "Death caused by misadventure. Tragic accident." There might be a connection between the death of this poor woman and that of Jacob.'

'The police inspector in Malvern, before I arrived, was a certain Alfred Robinson. According to the newspaper report, it seems that he was investigating the case. He lives in a small cottage on the Green in Colwall. I think we should pay him a visit. He may be able to tell us more about the case,' suggested Crabb.

'That is an excellent idea.'

* * *

Crabb pulled up the horse outside a small brick-built cottage situated on the Green in the Herefordshire village of Colwall. A grey-haired figure was busily engaged in digging in the garden at the front of the property.

Crabb assisted Lucy to alight from the trap.

'Good day to you,' said the man in the garden. 'You have come for the honey?

'The honey?' asked Crabb.

'I keep bees. Most of my visitors are here to buy honey.'

'I see. No, we do not require any honey. Are you Mr Robinson?' asked Crabb. 'We believe that you were in charge of Malvern Police Station some years ago?'

'That was so. How can I help you?' Robinson laid aside his fork.

'I am Constable Crabb from the station in Ledbury, and this lady is Mrs Ravenscroft, the wife of Detective Inspector Ravenscroft,' answered Crabb.

'Ravenscroft, you say? I've heard good things about your husband, madam. He has solved quite a few crimes in the area.'

'That is so,' said Lucy, smiling.

'I've been retired for past eight or nine years. I suspect you may be enquiring about one of my old cases.'

'Yes, sir. What do you recall about the death of Lizzie Warren?' asked Crabb.

'Lizzie Warren?' Robinson gave Crabb a cautious look.

'About ten years ago, up on Hangman Hill.'

'Oh yes. Poor woman. Found dead on the hills. It was my last case, about a month before I retired.'

'How did she die, Mr Robinson?' asked Lucy.

'She'd taken a nasty blow to the back of her head. She had fallen and hit the side of her head on one of the rocks. Been there for over a day when we found her. It was a sad way to go. I think she was only twenty or so,' muttered Robinson shaking his head.

'There was no suggestion that someone could have killed her?' said Crabb.

'No. Why ever would you think so?'

'These things are possible Mr Robinson,' replied the constable.

'Well, we did not suspect foul play. It was quite obvious to all of us that she had been out walking in the hills by herself when she fell and had this terrible accident.'

'There was no sign of any other injury?' asked Lucy.

'What other injury would you expect, Mrs Ravenscroft?'

'Something indicating that she might have been attacked in any way.'

'No, there was nothing of that nature.' Robinson picked up his fork again and resumed his digging.

'We believe that Lizzie worked on a farm called The Orchards out at Parkway. Did you interview the farmer?' asked Crabb.

'Yes, Constable, but we didn't get very far.'

'Oh? Why was that, sir?'

'Farmer there, man called Rostagon, was very surly and not very helpful. He told us that she had worked there on the farm for two or three years before her death, but that was all the information he gave us.'

'Did you find out anything else?' persisted Crabb.

'What do you mean — anything else?'

'Did Mr Rostagon say what Lizzie was doing up on the hills when she had her accident?'

'I don't remember. I suppose he said she had gone for a walk, or something like that.' Robinson thrust his fork into the ground. 'It was all such a long time ago. I don't know why you want to drag all this up again. No amount of questions or enquiries now will bring poor Lizzie back, will it?'

'There was a report?' asked Crabb.

'Of course there was a report, Constable. Look, I don't think there is anything else I can tell you about the case. It was just an unfortunate accident, and that's all there was to it. Now if you'll excuse me, I want to plant these seeds before the rains come,' said the former policeman.

'Well, thank you, Mr Robinson, we won't detain you any longer,' said Crabb, realising that any more questions would only cause annoyance, while probably adding nothing to what they knew already.

'Constable Crabb. Good day to you, Mrs Ravenscroft.'

'Good day to you, Mr Robinson,' said Lucy as she mounted the trap.

The retired policeman resumed his digging, as the trap made its way back on to the Wells Road.

'Well he wasn't able to provide us with much information,' said Crabb.

'It was all such a long time ago.'

'I am sure I would have remembered all the details of an incident like that for many years afterwards.'

'Tom, do you think we might have time to go out to Parkway before it gets dark?' asked Lucy. 'I'd like to see this Mr Rostagon.'

* * *

They continued their journey along the winding roads and over the railway line, the Malvern range always on their left, and past the Eastnor turn, until they eventually descended into the town of Ledbury. Here Crabb turned the horse sharply to the left on to the Gloucester road.

A few minutes later they arrived at the small hamlet of Parkway.

'I think the Orchards are this way,' said Crabb turning off to the left. The trap made its way up a rutted path that ran between fields of fruit trees and hops, before eventually pulling up at the entrance to a large farmhouse. As they arrived a barking sheepdog ran up towards them.

A heavily built man emerged from the inside a nearby stable and called the creature off. The dog snapped at Crabb before running over to its master.

'What do you want?' growled the man. His hair was untidy and he was unshaven, dressed in stained and muddy attire.

'I presume you are Mr Rostagon?'

'I am, and who wants him?' came back the curt reply.

'We are from the police station in Ledbury. I am Constable Crabb, and this lady is Mrs Ravenscroft, the wife of Detective Inspector Ravenscroft.'

'Since when have the police sent out their wives to make enquiries?' sneered the farmer.

'We are making enquiries concerning Lizzie Warren,' said Crabb. 'We understand that she was in your employ.'

The farmer paused for a moment before speaking. 'I told the police at the time all about it. That's all I've got to say. Now I've got the milking to get on with.'

107

'We understand that she met with an accident on the hills,' said Lucy.

'Well, if you knows that, what do you come bothering me for?' snapped Rostagon.

'Have a care, sir, remember you are speaking to a lady,' interjected Crabb.

'That's as may be. I'm done with all this. Michael! Michael!' yelled the farmer, turning on his heel.

'Perhaps we should go, Mrs Ravenscroft,' whispered Crabb.

'Michael! Where the blazes is that lazy good for nothing when you want him?'

At this, a middle-aged man emerged from the house.

'Ah, there you are,' went on Rostagon. 'These are the police, wanting to know all about Lizzie. You remember Lizzie. You tell 'em. I'm busy.' He and the dog disappeared into the barn.

'Lizzie?' enquired Michael, coming forward hesitantly.

'Yes. Lizzie Warren. I am Constable Crabb from Ledbury Police Station, and this is Mrs Ravenscroft, the wife of the Inspector,' said Crabb.

'But Lizzie, she been dead for over ten years,' stuttered Michael, a strained expression on his face.

'Can I ask your name and occupation, sir?' asked Crabb.

'Michael Sangster. I work for Mr Rostagon on the farm.'

'How long have you worked here?'

'Since I was a boy. Nearly twenty years.' He gave Crabb and Lucy a vacant stare.

'So you knew Lizzie Warren quite well?' continued Crabb.

'Yes, but she be dead.'

'I know. Can you tell us what happened on the day that Lizzie died?'

'I don't remember.' He turned away.

'It is very important Michael that we learn how Lizzie died,' said Lucy seeking to calm the labourer's anxiety.

'I don't remember,' mumbled Sangster.

'Please help us,' reiterated Lucy.

'It were after lunch on a Sunday, Lizzie said she was going for a walk. That were the last I saw of her.'

'Did she say where she was going?' asked Crabb.

'No. She went off towards Eastnor.'

'Did you go after her?'

'No.' He showed a sudden look of fear.

'That's alright, Michael,' said Lucy. 'We mean you no harm. Can you tell us anything else about Lizzie?'

'Lizzie was nice.'

'She was kind to you?' asked Lucy.

'Yes. She was always doing things for us. She helped me with my reading and writing.'

'That was very good of her.'

'I can write my name.'

'I am sure you can. Can you tell us, Michael, if anyone else other than Mr Rostagon, you, and Lizzie, worked on the farm at the time of her accident?' asked Lucy.

'No there was just the three of us. Master's wife, she died fifteen years ago.'

'What kind of work did Lizzie do?'

'She milked the cows, worked in the dairy, did the cooking.'

'Did Lizzie have a young man courting her?' continued Lucy.

'What you want to know that for?'

'I heard she was an attractive woman,' she hazarded. 'She must have had admirers?'

'There was only him.'

'Who was that?'

'Don't know.'

'Come, man, you must know who you mean,' said Crabb, finding that he was becoming irritated by the labourer's replies.

'Don't know.'

'How long had she known this man?' asked Lucy trying to encourage the labourer to be more forthcoming with his replies.

'I don't know,' muttered Sangster, staring vacantly down at the ground.

'She must have spoken about this man,' said Crabb.

Sangster did not reply.

'I don't think we can obtain anything further from this fellow, Mrs Ravenscroft.'

'Michael, was Lizzie going to meet that man on the day she went out to Eastnor?' asked Lucy.

'Don't know.'

'Are you sure about that?'

The labourer said nothing.

'If you can remember anything else, you can ask for me at the station in Ledbury,' Crabb told him.

'Jacob,' mumbled the labourer.

'What was that you said?' asked Crabb.

'Jacob. She said he was called Jacob.'

'Jacob!' exclaimed Lucy. 'She said she was going to meet Jacob?'

'Yes. It were Jacob.'

'Thank you,' said Lucy.

'Do you know what this means, Tom?' asked Lucy as the trap made its way down the lane.

'If it's the same Jacob, it means that the murdered man did indeed come from around these parts, and that Lizzie Warren was going to meet him in the hills, on that Sunday when she had the accident,' replied Crabb.

'This changes everything. I wonder whether Jacob could have played any part in Lizzie Warren's death?'

CHAPTER NINE

NEW YORK

Ravenscroft placed the knife and fork down on his plate.

'Food not to your liking, then?' enquired the young woman.

'I am not particularly hungry,' the detective lied.

'Suit yourself, then. It's your loss,' replied the woman, removing his plate. 'You want coffee?'

'Er . . . yes, please.'

Ravenscroft had entered the dining room of Ma Scrivens' Lodging House some sixty minutes earlier, having unwittingly slept for most of the day, to find it occupied by a dozen or so men, each of whom sat at a single table, in complete isolation from one another. He concluded that his fellow diners were all probably commercial travellers or clerks of a lower station in life. Each man had not communicated with any of the others during the meal, each having been busily engaged in reading what Ravenscroft supposed to be the local newspaper, in between courses.

The greasy soup, of a green appearance, Ravenscroft had found both unappetising and highly salty in taste, but at least it had been warm, and he had consumed half of its contents before deciding to abandon the effort. This had been followed by a plate of overcooked vegetables, anaemic-looking mashed potatoes, and a piece of meat which had been so tough in its texture that the detective would not have been surprised if someone had told him that it had originated from a labourer's leather boot.

'Coffee.' Interrupting his thoughts, the woman banged the tin mug down on the table before him, spilling some of the contents as she did so.

'Thank you. Tell me, have you worked here long?'

'Three weeks. What you want to know for?'

'No reason really, it was just that a friend of mine . . .' But before Ravenscroft could complete the sentence the woman had turned away and was busily serving the man at the next table.

Ravenscroft took a sip of the coffee, and found it surprisingly good. Turning towards the table that was nearest to him, he decided to break the silence of the room by addressing its occupant, a small, middle-aged, sour-looking man with a drooping moustache. 'Do you stay in this establishment very often?'

'Not if I can help it,' came back the curt reply.

Ravenscroft smiled. 'This is my first visit here.'

'Then I guess you won't be staying here again, buddy,' said the other without looking up from his paper.

'I guess not. May I ask why you stay here, then?' enquired Ravenscroft.

'It's cheap and convenient.'

'Have you been staying here long?'

'On and off, generally off, for the past five years. Why do you want to know?'

'A friend of mine was a resident here, but that was over ten years ago. I just wondered whether you might have remembered him.'

'I've been coming here for fifteen years,' said a voice from the other side of the room.

'Then perhaps you might recall my friend? His name was Thomas Temple. He was also an Englishman like myself,' replied Ravenscroft.

'The name means nothing to me.'

'Never heard of him,' joined in another voice.

Ravenscroft drank his coffee, and waited to see if anyone else in the room would be forthcoming, but he was met by a wall of silence and indifference.

'You want more coffee?' asked the woman returning to the room.

'Yes, thank you.'

Ravenscroft drank the rest of his coffee and made his way out of the dining room, colliding with a man in the hallway.

'I'm most terribly sorry,' apologised Ravenscroft.

'Think nothing of it,' said the tall dark-haired stranger, forcing a brief smile and raising his hat before turning the corner and quickly exiting the building.

'Might I have a word with Mrs Scrivens?' asked Ravenscroft, addressing the old man behind the reception desk.

'Leaving already? I knew you would. I said to Ma that you wouldn't last the day.'

'No, that is not so.'

'Us New Yorkers not good enough for you English, then?'

'That is not the case. I would just like a few words with the proprietor if you please.'

'What you want with Ma, then?'

'I would rather tell her, if you would be obliged,' said Ravenscroft, beginning to tire of the old man's abrasive manner.

'Ma! Ma!'

The door opened quickly. 'What you want? I'm busy,' growled the woman.

'Gent wants a word with you, Ma,' mumbled the man moving to the far end of the counter.

'Room not good enough for you, I suppose?'

'The room is just fine.'

'Then I suppose it's the food,' said the woman staring at Ravenscroft in a not entirely friendly way, as her ample bosom leaned threateningly over the edge of the counter.

'No, it is not the food.'

'What is it then?'

'I just require some information.'

'Information can be a dangerous thing in this town.'

'I believe a friend of mine, Thomas Temple, resided here. I just wondered whether you still remembered the gentleman at all?'

'Temple? You remember Temple?' the woman asked the clerk.

'I can't say as I do, Ma.'

'He was here about ten years ago,' continued Ravenscroft. 'He came over from England. He was the New York agent for a company called Mincing and Stricket.'

'What you want to know for?'

'He was a friend of mine in England, then he came over to New York, and I have not seen him since. I would rather like to make his acquaintance again, if at all possible,' said Ravenscroft, looking for the appropriate words and feeling increasingly uncomfortable.

'Temple!' laughed the old man.

'So you do remember him?'

'Oh yes, we remember him,' said Ma Scrivens drawing herself up to her full height, and folding her arms in a defensive posture.

'Well, can you tell me where I might find him?'

'Blackwell's. That's where you'll find him,' offered Ma.

'Blackwell's? Is that another lodging house?'

'Blackwell's a lodging house? Tell him, Ma,' laughed the old man.

'Blackwell's is a prison.'

'A prison!' exclaimed Ravenscroft. 'You mean Temple is in prison?'

'Yep — or rather, he was. He got sent down for two or three years, I think it was,' said Ma, forgetting her reticence.

'What was his crime?' asked a shocked Ravenscroft.

'Handling stolen goods. It was something to do with his work. I must say we were rather surprised. He always looked the type that would never hurt anybody. He was an English gent, not unlike you, I suppose,' sniffed the landlady.

'I see. Can you tell me more about this prison, Blackwell's?'

'It is on one of the islands.'

'How would I get there?'

'Take the ferry from East 26th Street.'

'Thank you. Was that the last you heard of him?' enquired Ravenscroft, anxious to capitalise on his questioning now that the couple were less guarded with their answers.

'Haven't seen him from the day he got sent down.'

'I don't suppose you know where the offices of Mincing and Stricket are?'

'Down by the docks. Write it down for you, if you like,' offered Ma, adopting a more helpful tone.

'That would be most kind of you. I will call upon them shortly.'

'That all?' enquired the old man, stroking his beard.

'Yes, thank you. I am most obliged for your assistance,' said Ravenscroft, accepting the scrap of paper from the landlady.

'I wouldn't go there this evening. It's getting dark now. It's not safe around that area, down by the docks,' said Ma.

Ravenscroft made his way back to his room, up the three flights of stairs. He had been startled by the news that Temple had been sent to prison. That would explain why he had broken off all contact with Mincing and Stricket in London. Now he knew where, and how, to reach the penitentiary, he resolved that the next morning, he would take the ferry across to the institution, and see if the authorities there could provide him with any more information regarding Maria Constantine's son.

115

Had Temple stolen goods from his employers? If so, why had not Mincing and Stricket mentioned this fact to Lucy when she had visited them in London? They had merely said that all contact with Temple had been lost. He wondered whether Mincing and Stricket had forgotten the real reason for not hearing from their employee, or whether they had been unwilling to disclose the truth. At least he now had the address of the warehouse. Perhaps people there would be more forthcoming about the fate of the former apprentice from the Foundling Hospital. He also wondered whether Temple might have changed his name to Jacob upon his release from the prison in order to hide his guilty past — but then he reminded himself that perhaps Temple and Jacob had been two different men rather than the same person.

As Ravenscroft lay down on his bed, he felt reassured that although he had not found Temple still living in Scrivens' Boarding House, he had at least two new avenues to explore in the morning, and that perhaps one of these places might lead him eventually to Temple himself.

* * *

Ravenscroft alighted from the cab at the quayside, and, fol-lowing the directions the cabman had given him, made his way down the cobbled street. On either side of him men were busy loading carts and wagons with parcels of goods from the warehouses, while others were securing large wooden crates to platforms that were being pulled up to openings situated on the upper floors of the buildings.

Reaching the end of the quay, Ravenscroft turned to his right and found that he was walking along a narrower, darker and quieter alleyway that ran alongside the water. After a few hundred yards, an old warehouse came into view, and as he drew nearer he was rewarded by the words 'Mincing and Stricket' in faded letters on the side of the building.

He made his way up a flight of old wooden steps, which had clearly seen better days, as each one creaked loudly with

the sound of his feet, whereas others were in such a state of
disrepair that Ravenscroft could see the ground below him
in several places where the wood had decayed. Eventually
reaching a small landing at the top of the flight, he was disappointed to find that the door was tightly secured with a large
padlock. As he looked up at the grime-coloured windows,
and surveyed the state of the neglected building, he wondered whether the premises had been left vacant for many
years. The New York operation of Mincing and Stricket
must have ceased with Temple's conviction. Frustrated that
he had come this far, and that this line of enquiry had come
to nothing, Ravenscroft retraced his way carefully down the
rotting staircase. Perhaps there was another entrance to the
building located round the corner, but again a brick wall
thwarted him.

The noise of a cab drawing up outside the main entrance
startled him, and Ravenscroft instinctively peered round the
corner to see who the new arrival was.

'You need not wait,' said a familiar voice, and the cab
departed.

The fellow walking across to the steps was none other
than Mr Petters, who he had met on the *Etruria*. The detective drew further back round the building so that he could
observe the new arrival without giving away his own presence. He watched as the man walked up the steps and took
out a key from his pocket to open the padlock on the door,
before entering the warehouse.

Ravenscroft's first instinct was to climb the steps, to
enter and declare himself to Petters, but then he remembered the warning he had been given on the ship, and
decided to remain hidden. He knew that Petters was one
of O'Callaghan's associates. Now it seemed as though these
men had some connection with Mincing and Stricket. Had
they also known Temple, and if so had the poor unfortunate
Englishman been implicated in some unlawful activity in
which they had all been complicit? Had Temple changed his
name to Jacob after his time in prison and eventually made

his way back to England? O'Callaghan and his associates had returned to New York on the *Etruria* — what was their business in England? Could they have tracked down Jacob, and strung up his body on Hangman Hill, perhaps because he had betrayed them all those years ago? All these thoughts seemed to tumble into his mind in quick succession, and the more he thought about the matter, the more unanswered questions seemed to present themselves.

The noise of footsteps on the creaking boards alerted him to the fact that Petters was now leaving the warehouse. He peered round the corner and saw that Petters was carrying what appeared to be a brown paper parcel. He walked back up the narrow alleyway and out of sight.

Ravenscroft waited for two or three minutes before he ventured forth. A quick glance up to the landing showed him that Petters had again secured the padlock.

He wondered what was inside the old warehouse. Although the building did not look as though it had been used for years, it nevertheless must have contained some items of worth, as Petters had collected a parcel from inside.

His curiosity had been aroused, and he knew that he would need to gain access to the interior of the building and make a search of the premises. He decided that he would return later, when darkness had fallen, and see what secrets the warehouse held.

* * *

Ravenscroft boarded the ferry, and looked out across the East River as the vessel began to make the short crossing to Blackwell's Island.

'You visiting someone there?' enquired one of the old seamen.

'Yes,' replied Ravenscroft.

'Better than staying there, I would be bound.'

'Yes, I would not wish to do that.'

'Do you see those buildings over there? They house nearly two thousand prisoners.'

'That is rather a lot for such a small island.'

'And that building to the side is the workhouse.'

'So the poor and infirm live there as well as the criminal classes?'

'Sure do.'

'Is that a lighthouse at the northern point?'

'Sure is. It must be hard for the poor devils inside, to look out of their cell windows and see the waters and the houses across the river, and realise what they have lost.'

'Indeed. Have any of the prisoners ever escaped?'

'They do from time to time, but they don't get very far. If the river does not get them, the law usually catches up with them before long. You are not from around these parts then?'

'No. I am from England.'

'England. That's a long way to have come.'

'It is indeed.'

'Ferry will be there in a few minutes. The return trip is on the hour, every hour till dusk.'

'Thank you. You have been most informative.'

A few minutes later, Ravenscroft alighted from the ferry. He looked up at the austere uniform buildings ahead, and decided to make his way up the cobbled pathway towards the central block. As he passed a group of men dressed in prison uniforms who were busily engaged in laying bricks for the foundations of a new building, one of the warders raised his cap in acknowledgement.

'Good morning,' said Ravenscroft. 'Can you tell me if I am going in the right direction to the main office?'

'Indeed, sir, just follow the path to the front door over there,' replied the warder, pointing.

Upon reaching the front entrance Ravenscroft pushed open the door and entered a large hallway.

'Can I help you, sir?' asked a clerk coming forward to meet him.

'Good morning. My name is Detective Inspector Ravenscroft, from England. I would like to speak with the Warden if I may? Perhaps you would be good enough to give him my card.'

'You have come rather a long way,' sniffed the clerk, accepting the card. 'If you would care to take a seat over there, sir, I will ascertain whether the Warden will see you.'

Ravenscroft watched as the clerk made his way up a winding staircase, before seating himself on one of the straight-backed chairs. As he looked around the hall he observed a number of paintings on the walls and deduced that each of them was probably a portrait of one of the previous wardens.

After a few minutes he was rewarded by the sight of a grey-haired elderly gentleman making his way down the stairs, the clerk following on behind him.

'Good morning. Your card says that you are Detective Inspector Ravenscroft from England.'

'That is indeed so.'

'It is not every day that we have a visit from a policeman from England. I hope you are not checking up on all us errant Yankees? We did obtain our independence over a hundred years ago,' laughed the Warden.

'Indeed you did, sir, and from what I have seen of New York so far, you seem to be making a good job of it.'

'That is kind of you to say so, Inspector Ravenscroft. Now how can I be of assistance to you?'

'I would like some information regarding one of your previous inmates.'

'One of our past inmates, you say? Then I think you had better come into the office where we keep all our records.'

Ravenscroft followed the Warden into a large room that lead off the hall.

'What name are you looking for?' said the Warden, sitting down in a large leather armchair.

'The name of the prisoner was Thomas Temple. I believe he was sentenced to two or three years' imprisonment here, approximately ten years ago,' said Ravenscroft, accepting the seat that had been indicated.

'Finch, if you will be so good,' the Warden addressed the clerk.

'Yes, sir.' The young man busily opened a number of cabinets at the side of the room.

'May I ask what your interest in Temple is?' asked the Warden, leaning back in his chair, and arching his fingers beneath his chin as he stared at Ravenscroft.

'A few weeks ago, a man was murdered near the town where I live. He had been strung up from a tree. At first we were unable to identify him, but our enquiries eventually led us to your city. The landlady of the house where Temple resided told me of Temple's crime and sentence.'

'Forgive me Inspector Ravenscroft, but why have you come all this way for a man who is dead? I would have thought that your detective skills would have been put to better use in your own country?'

'I know that this may seem strange, but we are not certain that the dead man was indeed called Thomas Temple. I have to find out what happened to him when he came to America, so as I can ascertain whether he was the victim, or someone who was involved in his murder.'

'I see. The name Thomas Temple means nothing to me, but I only came to the island three years ago, and young Finch here has only been with us for less than a year.'

'Fifteen months, sir,' interjected the clerk, placing a folder on the desk.

'Fifteen months. I stand corrected, Finch. Now let us see what we have here — "Thomas Temple. Born England; sentenced to two years' and three months' imprisonment for dealing in stolen goods. Prisoner showed Good Conduct; released on time." I am afraid that is all it says.'

'There is no photograph?'

'No. We do sometimes take photographs of our prisoners, but I am afraid there does not appear to be one here.'

'I wonder whether it would be possible to discover what happened to Temple when he left the prison?' asked Ravenscroft, somewhat disappointed.

'Well yes, I think we might be able to assist you there. There is a note made in pencil to say that Temple secured employment at Macy and Co.'

'What is that?'

'Macy's is a New York department store.'

'I see. Forgive me, but is it usual practice for the penitentiary to secure employment for its prisoners upon their release?'

'Not usually, but as the note was made by my predecessor I can only conclude that this was some kind of special case. Perhaps he felt that your man Temple was deserving of a new start in life, and somehow used his influence in securing the position for him.'

'That is most interesting. Is there anything else in the prisoner's file that may be of interest?'

'No, it would appear as though Temple was a model prisoner. Macy's is an important department store here in New York. It would not have taken on Temple lightly. I have no doubt that the Warden's personal recommendation helped in this case.'

'So it would appear. Thank you both for your assistance,' said Ravenscroft rising from his seat.

'I am glad that we have been able to help you. What will you do now, Inspector?'

'Follow the trail to Macy's,' replied Ravenscroft. 'I would be obliged if you could tell me where I might find the store?'

'Of course. Macy and Co. is on 18th Street.'

* * *

Later that afternoon Ravenscroft looked up at the sign above the doorway of a large building which bore the letters 'R. H. Macy and Co.' Inside, long shop counters ran the length of the cavernous room, along the walls and down the centre.

'Can I help you, sir?' said a doorman.

'Yes, I require some information about your store. Might I speak with someone who may be able to assist me in my quest?'

'Certainly, come with me, sir.'

Ravenscroft followed the doorman down the aisle of busy shoppers towards a central staircase.

'Gentleman would like to speak with someone in authority,' said the doorman addressing a thin, tall lady standing by one of the counters.

'And what is the nature of your enquiry, sir?' asked the lady.

'I am an English policeman. I require some information regarding one of your employees. Perhaps I could have a word with the manager of the store?'

'Certainly, sir. If you would care to follow me.'

Ravenscroft followed the assistant up a flight of stairs.

'Gentleman to see the manager,' said the assistant, addressing a young woman at the top of the staircase.

'Oh my, do please follow me, sir,' said the woman, smiling.

Ravenscroft followed her up the next flight of steps.

'I guess you are from not from around these parts?' asked the woman.

'Your assumption is correct. I have come from England.'

'England! My, how quaint is that!' she giggled. 'English gentleman to see Mr Gordon,' she said to a more elderly serious woman at the top of the stairs.

'Good morning,' said Ravenscroft.

'He's from England.' She gave Ravenscroft a broad smile before skipping down the stairs.

'Please follow me, sir,' said the more serious shop assistant.

As Ravenscroft followed this new attendant through the aisle of counters and up another two flights of stairs he was beginning to wonder whether he would ever arrive at his destination.

'English gentleman to see Mr Gordon,' said the woman addressing a young clerk.

'Would you care to follow me, sir,' said the young man.

Ravenscroft thanked the female assistant, and followed the young man up a further two flights of stairs, then along a brightly painted corridor until they reached a closed door.

'I will see if someone can assist you, sir.' He knocked on the door.

'Yes, Murray?' asked an elderly man opening the door.

'Gentleman would like a word with Mr Gordon, sir.'

'Well I'm afraid that won't be possible. Mr Gordon is very busy at the present. He cannot possibly see anyone today. You should not have brought the gentleman up here.'

'Forgive me,' said Ravenscroft stepping forward and taking out his card from his coat pocket. 'My name is Detective Inspector Ravenscroft. I have come all the way from England, on a most urgent matter.'

'You should have written first; could have saved you the journey,' replied the man in a lofty manner.

'It is most imperative that I have a word with the manager. It concerns one of your employees,' persisted the detective. 'I will not take up more than a few minutes of your manager's time.'

The man studied the card. 'Wait here.' He abruptly closed the door in Ravenscroft's face.

Murray looked upwards, then smiled and shuffled his feet, as Ravenscroft felt himself becoming more and more frustrated.

'He's very busy,' remarked Murray after a full minute had elapsed.

'I see,' sighed Ravenscroft.

'Sorry, Mr Gordon is far too busy today,' said the elderly clerk, opening the door once more. 'You will have to make an appointment. Perhaps he will see you next week.'

'I do not have the time to make an appointment,' Ravenscroft's voice rose. 'Will you kindly inform Mr Gordon that this is a very important criminal matter, and that it is imperative that I see him without delay.'

'No need for annoyance, sir.'

'Then please tell your Mr Gordon that I must see him now.'

'What's all that noise, Fothergill?' boomed a voice from within.

Ravenscroft seized the opportunity and quickly brushed past the elderly clerk and strode into the office.

'You can't go in there,' protested Fothergill.

'What the blazes is going on?' said a fat, red-faced man who was seated behind a large desk at the rear of the room.

'Forgive the intrusion, sir, but I must have words with you on a most urgent matter,' began Ravenscroft.

'I am sorry, Mr Gordon, I did tell the gentleman that you were otherwise engaged,' stuttered Fothergill.

'Oh, it is of no matter. Detective, it says here,' said Gordon looking at Ravenscroft's card. 'You are from England as well. Hell, you sure have come a long way, mister.'

'I have indeed.'

'Well I suppose I can give you two minutes. Time is money, you know.'

'Indeed.'

'Well, get on with it, then.'

'I am investigating a murder that took place a few weeks ago in England. We have reason to believe that one of your employees is implicated in the murder. His name is Thomas Temple,' said Ravenscroft, anxious to condense his request into as few words as possible.

'Name means nothing to me. Temple, you say? Look out his file, Fothergill.'

Gordon resumed his writing, as the clerk searched through a large cabinet in the corner of the room, muttering aloud as he did so.

'You have a most impressive store here,' said Ravenscroft attempting to break the silence.

'Macy's is the best in New York.'

'I expect so.'

'I say so,' emphasised Gordon. 'Soon all the cities in the world will be full of these stores. You have a store like this in your town in England?'

'No, we only have small shops.'

'Well, you mark my word, it won't be long before there is one.'

'I very much doubt that,' smiled Ravenscroft.

'London should take a leaf out of our book, and build department stores. The day of the small shop is over,' said Gordon, lighting up a large cigar.

'The file, sir,' said Fothergill placing a folder on his superior's desk.

'Now let us see what we have here.' Gordon opened the file and began to read. '"Thomas Temple: Born England; period of employment, June 1884 until August 1885. Employed in China Department." That's all. No, wait a moment. "Reason for termination of employment — employee wished to return to home country."'

'He returned to England!' exclaimed Ravenscroft.

'That's what it says here, in black and white.'

'It does not say how he obtained employment in your store?'

'No.'

'You do not have a photograph of Mr Temple, by any chance?' asked Ravenscroft, disappointed.

'No.'

'And there is nothing else in the file, about his conduct or his appearance?'

'No. The rest of the file is empty.'

'He must have been quite an impressive young man,' interjected Fothergill.

'Oh, why do you say that?' asked Ravenscroft.

'China is our most lucrative department. Nearly a third of all our sales come from the china department. We tend to place the most presentable of our staff in that section,' answered Fothergill.

'I see.'

'Well if that is all Mr . . . er?'

'Ravenscroft.'

'Inspector Ravenscroft. You must excuse me. Time is important to us all here at Macy's,' said Gordon resuming his writing.

Fothergill coughed, and Ravenscroft realising that nothing more could be gained by prolonging the interview, rose from his chair.

'Enjoy your time in New York, Inspector Ravenscroft. Hope you catch who you are after,' said Gordon, without looking up from his papers.

'Thank you,' answered Ravenscroft as he made his way towards the door.

'Why not buy the little lady at home something pretty on your way out of the store?' shouted Gordon as Ravenscroft closed the door behind him.

* * *

Later that evening Ravenscroft paid off the cabman. As he began to walk down the cobbled street at the side of the docks his thoughts turned to what he had discovered earlier that day. The trail had led him from Ma Scrivens' Lodging House, to the penitentiary on Blackwell's Island where he had learned of Temple's criminal record, and then on to Macy's Department Store, and all the time he had thought that he was getting nearer to his quarry, but then had come the final blow that Thomas Temple had left New York and returned to England some six years previous. He had come all this way in the hope of finding Temple, only to discover that the man was no longer resident in the city. The trail had come to an abrupt end. There would be nothing else for it but to return home and tell Maria Constantine that he was no closer to knowing the whereabouts of her son.

Other than the note in Macy's file, Ravenscroft had no proof that Temple had indeed returned to England. The fact that he had seen the man Petters collecting a parcel from the former warehouse of Mincing and Stricket earlier that day, and that he had learned that Temple had worked for that company before being sent to prison for 'receiving stolen goods' strongly suggested that Temple had been an associate of O'Callaghan. Could Temple have lied when he had left Macy's? Perhaps he had not returned to England at all, but had resumed his criminal activities with this New York gang?

The more he thought about the case, the more he was convinced that he had to know what was inside that warehouse. The answers to all his questions were there. There might be records inside that would tell him more about Temple's whereabouts, and if he could find evidence of O'Callaghan's criminal activities he could then go to the police authorities in New York.

To break into the building in daylight risked his being discovered by anyone who happened to be walking past the premises. But if he were to enter when it was dark he would need a lantern to light his way, and he then risked that the bright light would draw attention. Finally, he had decided to return to the warehouse as the afternoon light was fading, when the area would probably be quieter, and yet there would be enough light to enable him to find his way into the building.

Reaching the bottom of the steps, Ravenscroft looked hastily behind him. Being satisfied that there was no one present, he climbed the old creaking stairs and forced the padlock from its fixture. The door was still locked, so he placed his shoulder against the rotting woodwork and was rewarded by the ease with which the door gave way.

He stood for some minutes in what at first sight appeared to be an empty room, but after a few seconds his eyes adjusted to the gloomy interior and he observed a table and some shelves at the far end.

On the desk lay a large number of papers. Ravenscroft thumbed through the pile, straining to see the writing on some of the pages, but could not make sense of any of the contents. He then turned his attention to the shelves located to either side of the desk. Here, several wooden packing cases were stacked. He moved some of the cases, which were not heavy, but could find no writing on the outside to suggest what lay inside. Taking one of the wooden boxes over towards the desk, he prised open the top. He peered into the case, and felt about in the packing straw. He withdrew his hand, to discover he was clutching a collection of necklaces, rings and other fine jewellery.

'I think you should put that back inside the box, Mr Ravenscroft!'

Ravenscroft turned quickly and found that he was staring into the bright light of a lantern. Shielding his eyes from the glare, he made out the figure of Petters pointing a gun in his direction.

'Dear, dear me, Mr Ravenscroft, what do we have here?'

Ravenscroft recognised the voice of O'Callaghan, and as the American came into view he also noticed the man Foy, and one or two other men who were unknown to him.

'We thought you might return. Mr Petters here noticed you looking around outside earlier today. You should have been more careful. Curiosity is a dangerous thing, Mr Ravenscroft. Tie him to the chair, Foy,' instructed O'Callaghan.

Two of the men seized Ravenscroft and rudely thrust him into the chair, as Foy wrapped a rope tightly round his legs and arms.

'Well, Mr Ravenscroft, just who are you?' O'Callaghan took a pull on a large cigar. 'We don't believe all that nonsense about butterflies.'

'It's the truth. I am a butterfly collector,' protested Ravenscroft, knowing that the men were unlikely to believe him.

'I'll make him talk,' growled Foy, drawing out a nasty-looking metal object from his pocket.

'He'll be in the pay of them damn Pinkertons,' added Foy.

'I tell you, I am nothing to do with any of the authorities. I have come to your country for peaceful purposes,'
Ravenscroft persisted, the sweat breaking out on his brow.

'Let me do him over,' threatened Foy, edging closer. 'I'll
enjoy cutting him into little pieces.'

'Wait!' shouted O'Callaghan. 'I want to know what he
has been up to. There could be more of them. You might as
well tell us the truth, Mr Ravenscroft. Mr Foy here can be
very persuasive, I can assure you, and it will save you a lot
of pain.'

Foy waved the implement and Ravenscroft gulped.
Perhaps it was better to come clean, as O'Callaghan said.

'Alright,' he began, 'I'm an English detective.'

'I knew it!' said Foy. 'Let me finish him off now!'

'The authorities know that I am here.'

'Don't make me laugh,' said O'Callaghan blowing
smoke into Ravenscroft's face. 'No one knows you are here.
After we have finished with you, you will be thrown into the
harbour, where you will sink to the bottom of the sea, and
be eaten by the fishes. Your people at home will never know
how you died.'

'Is that what you did to Temple all those years ago?'

'Temple? What's he on about? Damn Englishman,'
growled Petters.

'I have only come to New York to find out what happened to Thomas Temple. He used to work in this building;
that's why I am here. I am not interested in your activities,'
pleaded Ravenscroft.

'Too late for that now, Mr Ravenscroft!' snapped
O'Callaghan. 'You should not have wandered in here tonight.
That was such a foolish thing to do. We cannot possibly let
you go now. You know too much about our operation.'

'What operation? I don't know anything at all.' Ravenscroft
realised that he was pleading for his life. 'Look, I am sure we can
come to some arrangement.'

'Arrangement!' O'Callaghan sneered. 'You English,
always the same, so damned polite. We don't need to come

130

to any "arrangement". You are a stupid man, Ravenscroft, and your stupidity will now be the death of you. You should have kept out of our affairs. I'm bored by all this. Shoot him, Foy, and then throw him into the river!'

'Please, don't do this,' pleaded Ravenscroft, thinking of Lucy and his children.

'Foy!' commanded O'Callaghan.

Ravenscroft closed his eyes.

A shot rang out!

CHAPTER TEN

HEREFORDSHIRE

'Ravenscroft here?'

Crabb looked up from behind the desk in Ledbury Police Station.

'Are you deaf, Constable? I asked if Ravenscroft was here?' said the tall broad-whiskered man, before Crabb could answer.

'I am afraid the Inspector is away at present, sir.'

'When will he be back?'

'I am unable to say,' replied Crabb.

'"Unable to say" — what kind of answer is that?' growled the new arrival.

'I am sorry, but it is the only answer I can give at the moment. The inspector is out of the country, and we don't know when he will return.'

'Well that's damned inconvenient. Damned inconvenient. Who are you, then?'

'I am Constable Crabb. I am in charge during the Inspector's absence,' smiled Crabb, hoping to placate the aggressive newcomer, but realising that he would probably not succeed.

'Damn it! I suppose you'll have to do then,' replied the other grudgingly. 'I wish to report a burglary.'

'May I take down some details?' said Crabb reaching for his pencil.

'Colonel Wendover. Army. Retired.'

'I assume that it is your house that has been burgled, Colonel?'

'You assume correctly, Constable.'

'When did this burglary take place?'

'Don't rightly know.'

'You don't rightly know?' asked Crabb.

'Don't repeat everything that I say, man!'

'I'm sorry, sir. Could I have your address?'

'Ashanti, Much Marcle.'

'Ashanti is a rather unusual name for a house, if I may say so,' remarked Crabb, writing down the details.

'Ashanti's where I fought the blighters in '73.'

'I see. You say that you are not certain when the burglary took place?'

'My wife and I have been away for the past four weeks. Been taking the air and all that in Eastbourne. House has been closed up. It was only when we returned yesterday that we discovered a burglary had taken place during our absence.'

'I see. Was much damage committed?'

'The safe was broken into. The damn blighters took my wife's jewellery, my medals and fifty pounds that were all inside. I tell you, if I get hold of them they won't be able to sit down for a year!'

'Was anything else taken from the house?'

'No, they seem to have left everything else. Good job they didn't get the Ming vases. Went straight for the safe, they did.'

'Would you be able to provide me with a list of items that were taken?'

'Wrote them down here.' Wendover produced a piece of paper from his pocket and slapped it down on the counter.

'Thank you, sir.' Crabb picked up the list and studied its contents.

'Now, what I want to know is: what are you going to do about it?'

'You say the house was shut up during your stay in Eastbourne? May I ask if you have any servants?'

'Yes, Roberts, he is my man. He came with us. I sent the housekeeper and maid away for the month.'

'Have they been with you long?'

'Yes. Ah, see what you are getting at; inside job and all that. Sorry to disappoint you, Constable. Roberts has been with me for over twenty years. He was my batman during my army days. He is entirely loyal. Mrs Glencoe, the housekeeper, has been with us since we moved here fifteen years ago, and Mary the maid for five years. If any of them wanted to rob me, they would have done it long ago. Barking up the wrong tree there, I'm afraid.'

'Did anyone unknown to you call at the house before you left for Eastbourne?' asked Crabb, trying to think of all the questions he should ask.

'No, can't recall anyone.'

'I see.'

'What do you mean "I see"? Stop saying that; it is damned annoying. I want to know what you are going to do about it? My wife was very attached to her jewels, and my medals can't be replaced. Damn the devils!'

'I will come over this afternoon and inspect the damage.'

'Huh, a fat lot of good that will do. Whoever broke into my safe knew what they were up to.'

'I agree, sir, but it will help our enquiries if I could see the scene of the crime,' said Crabb laying down his pencil on the counter.

'I suppose it will do no harm.' Wendover pulled a sour face.

'I will also circulate your list of stolen items to other police stations in the area, and make enquiries at jewellers in Ledbury, Hereford and Worcester.'

'You think the scoundrels will try to sell them so close to where they committed the crime?'

'It is possible. Thieves will often try to either sell or pawn items they have stolen as quickly as they can.'

'Right, Constable, I will see you sharpish this afternoon. I want our possessions found.'

'I will endeavour to do my best for you.'

Wendover nodded and strode briskly out of the office.

* * *

Later that afternoon, Crabb closed the door of Ashanti in the Herefordshire village of Much Marcle, having just viewed the scene of the robbery. He had reassured both Colonel Wendover and his distressed wife that he would do all he could to recover their lost property. Now he decided to walk into the village, and as he drew near to the medieval church he greeted an old man cutting grass at the edge of the road.

'Good day to ye, Constable.' The gardener paused from his labours and wiped his brow. 'Dear me, 'tis hard work, this cutting. I be all of a swither. You has been to the Colonel's, no doubt?'

'I have, indeed.'

'It were a bad thing, that burglary. The Colonel didn't deserve that. It's a sad state of affairs if a man and his wife can't go away from their home without it being burgled like that.'

'Indeed. News travels fast.'

'There's nothing that goes on in Much Marcle that I don't know about,' grinned the man.

'Can you tell me whether you have seen any strangers in the area during the past month or so?' asked Crabb.

'No. I don't think so. There was only that fellow who put that poster yonder some weeks ago.' He pointed to a tree outside the church.

'What poster?' asked Crabb.

'Why, that poster that were advertising the fair in Ledbury. I don't hold with fairs much. Waste of both money and time, if you asks me.'

'I wonder if you could describe this man for me?' asked Crabb, taking out his notebook.

'Two of them, there were. There was the tall one. Bit of a noddy, he were. He had a long white beard. I remember he had a brightly coloured yellow waistcoat. Bit of a show-off, if you ask me, wearing a waistcoat like that. 'E's a faddy and no mistake,' replied the man, warming to his subject.

'Can you tell me what the other fellow looked like?'

'He were younger than the other one, that's all I can say about him. Tell you the truth, I didn't take too much notice of them. They weren't 'ere long. They were in a bit of a hespil.'

'Hespil?' asked Crabb looking up from his notebook.

'Yes, hespil; you know? They were in a hurry.'

'I see. Well thank you for your information.'

'Glad to have been of assistance. We must all help the law.'

Crabb returned to the trap deep in thought. After a moment's deliberation he urged the horse forward.

* * *

'Good day to you, Constable Crabb,' said the cheery-faced police officer. 'What brings you to Hereford? Inspector Ravenscroft is not with you?'

'No, the inspector is away, in America.'

'America? What's his nibs doing there?'

'He is following up a possible line of enquiry.'

'It seems a long way to go on an enquiry. Wish they would send me to America on police business. Still, some folks have all the luck. So Ravenscroft has left you in charge, has he?'

'Yes, Sergeant Morris.'

'And what can we do for you, my lad?'

'I have just visited Much Marcle. Gentleman by the name of Wendover has had his house broken into and several items taken — jewellery, medals, money — while he was away. Have you had any similar burglaries in your area?' asked Crabb.

'Let me see.' The sergeant consulted a large ledger on his desk. 'Ah yes, big house just outside Hereford was burgled some weeks ago. Some items of jewellery were taken.'

'When was this?'

'Sometime in early October I think.'

'I knew it!' exclaimed Crabb. 'Tell me, Sergeant, do you recall if the travelling fair was here at that same time?'

'Let's have a look. Ah, yes, it was the same week. I see that several arrests were made for drunkenness and disorderly conduct at the fair. Why lad? You think there's a connection?' Sergeant Morris looked up at Crabb.

'The Much Marcle burglary probably took place when the fair was in Ledbury. A villager there recollects seeing two men from the fair putting up posters near the house.'

'And you think these men from the fair were on the lookout for properties which were unoccupied?'

'Yes.'

'You could well be on to something there, Constable Crabb.'

'After the fair left Ledbury it went on to Tewkesbury.'

'Wait here, lad.' Sergeant Morris disappeared into the next room, before returning a few seconds later holding a collection of papers. 'Tewkesbury, you say? I remember reading about something — yes, here we are, a report of a burglary at a house along the Gloucester road just outside the town.'

'When did that take place, Sergeant?' asked Crabb, consulting his notebook.

'About a week after the fair left here.'

'And after it had been to Ledbury.' Crabb grew animated. 'After Tewkesbury, I believe the fair went on to Evesham.'

'Yes here we are, Constable, similar breaking and entering just outside Evesham a few days later.'

'There you have it!' exclaimed Crabb. 'Shortly before the fair arrives in a town, Mr Rockstone and his accomplice go round the nearby areas, putting up posters, and looking out for empty properties that they can enter after it is dark and everyone has gone to the fair.'

'Sorry, but who is this Mr Rockstone?' asked a perplexed Morris.

'He is the fellow we have been seeking in connection with the hanging on the Malvern Hills. He is a showman, selling quack medicines at the fair.'

'I remember reading about the murder in the local newspaper. Nobody seemed to know the name of the dead man. Where is Mr Rockstone now?'

'I am afraid we don't know. We have been searching everywhere for him.'

'Well I must congratulate you, Constable Crabb, on an excellent piece of criminal deduction.'

'Thank you, Sergeant.'

'What we need to do now, is find out where that fair of yours is at the present time. The fact that these burglaries have continued after the fair left Ledbury, suggests to me that Mr Rockstone has returned to his companions.'

'I think you are correct, Sergeant.'

'Find the whereabouts of this fair, keep them under observation, and catch them in the act. We will have them, lad!' Sergeant Morris rubbed his hands enthusiastically. 'We will have this Rockstone fellow. Yes we will. I say again, well done to you Constable Crabb.'

* * *

'Good morning, Mr Clifford,' said Lucy, entering The Malvern Reading Rooms.

'Good morning to you, Mrs Ravenscroft,' replied the librarian, giving a little bow. 'May I say how pleasant it is to see you again.'

'Thank you, Mr Clifford.'

'I trust your husband is well?'

'As far as I know.'

'I believe that you may be after further information?'

'Indeed. You may recall that when Constable Crabb and I visited you last week, you were able to show us the newspaper report concerning the death of Lizzie Warren.'

'Yes. You would like to see the report again?'

'If I may, I would be most obliged.'

'Please follow me, my good lady.'

Lucy followed the librarian into the back room.

'If you would care to take a seat, I will bring over the volume for you,' smiled Clifford.

'Thank you.' Lucy removed her gloves and sat at the table.

'I think this was the volume,' said Clifford after a few moments had elapsed. 'If you will excuse me, I will have to leave you to your own devices, as I believe another customer may have just entered the library.'

Lucy opened the large volume as the librarian departed the room, and began to turn over the pages until she found the report of Lizzie Warren's death. As she read again the words describing the tragedy on the hills, she recalled the farm at Parkway that she and Tom Crabb had visited, where the unfortunate woman had worked, and from where she had last been seen by Michael Sangster on that fateful morning walking out towards the hills.

She turned over the pages where she again found the report of the inquest — 'Death Caused by Misadventure'. Had Lizzie Warren died as the result of a fall on Hangman Hill, or had Jacob been involved in her death? Sangster had said that Lizzie was being courted by Jacob. Had the lovers met up on the hill? If so, had they quarrelled with the result that Jacob had killed Lizzie? If that had been the case, it would also explain why Jacob had been unwilling to return to the area where the tragedy had taken place.

Lucy turned the pages of the newspaper, but could find no further mention of the case in that week's issue. Turning to the next weekly issue, she was surprised to see the entry she had been seeking.

FUNERAL OF LIZZIE WARREN

The funeral took place last Thursday morning, at Little Malvern Priory, of Lizzie Warren, who had met with a tragic accident on Hangman Hill. We understand that no relatives were present at the service and burial, as it appears that the poor unfortunate woman was quite alone in this world. Mourners included Lizzie Warren's employer, Mr S. Rostagon of The Orchards, Parkway, and Mr Michael Sangster, a fellow employee. Also present were Mr Francis Constantine of The Verzons, Trumpet near Ledbury, and . . .

Lucy sat back in her chair in dismay.

Why had Francis Constantine attended Lizzie Warren's funeral?

The Orchards and The Verzons were several miles apart, so he could not have attended the funeral out of respect as a near neighbour. What had been the connection between the Herefordshire landowner and the milkmaid from Parkway?

Had Francis Constantine played some part in the death of Lizzie Warren on the top of Hangman Hill, on that fateful Sunday morning all those years ago?

CHAPTER ELEVEN

NEW YORK

'Drop your weapons and put your hands up in the air!' shouted out an unfamiliar voice.

'Damn it! Pinkertons!' exclaimed O'Callaghan.

Ravenscroft opened his eyes and looked towards the entrance where a group of men had just rushed into the room. There was a crash as O'Callaghan dropped the lantern, and a rushing of feet and shouting as the place was plunged into darkness and chaos.

'Grab hold of them, men! Don't let any of them get away,' instructed the first voice.

Ravenscroft strained to see what was going on in the room, but all he could see in the gloom were groups of men fighting and crashing into each other as various cries and shouts went on.

'Soon have you free, Inspector Ravenscroft,' said the owner of the first voice. His rescuer bent down and began untying the rope, as one or two lanterns were lit.

'Who are you?' stuttered Ravenscroft. He was shaking with relief and anxiety.

'Bill Richardson, of Pinkerton Detective Agency, at your service,' replied the man.

'I saw you in the boarding house. You are the fellow I collided with in the hallway,' said Ravenscroft, rubbing his wrists where the rope had bitten into the flesh.

'Sure did.'

'You have been following me?'

'Sure have — Blackwell's Penitentiary, Macy's Department Store. You have been a busy man, Inspector Ravenscroft.'

'But why?'

'Well, we have been after these fellows for years. Once you were observed dining with O'Callaghan and his men we couldn't be sure that you were not implicated in their crooked network, so the best thing we could do was to keep you under observation.'

'I assure you that I was not involved in their crooked affairs.'

'I can see that now. Sorry we couldn't rescue you before, but we were hoping you would lead us to these crooks, as I am sure you will appreciate.'

'Well I am mighty glad that you arrived just in time. Another second and I would have been dead. You were also on the *Etruria*?'

'Sure were. You were getting mighty close to O'Callaghan and his associates.'

'So it was you who sent me the warning note?'

'Guilty as charged,' laughed Richardson.

'You were travelling back from England. It must have been you who took those photographs from out of my drawer in Ledbury?'

'I guess you will have to charge me with breaking and entering.'

'And you destroyed the photographic plates at Lancing's studio?'

'Yes. I must say I feel rather bad about that. Before you leave New York, I will make a payment to the gentleman, which you can give to him, to cover the cost of the damage caused.'

'But why? Why did you take the photographs of Jacob? What were you trying to conceal?' asked Ravenscroft. He was still shaky after his ordeal, but he had to know.

'That's a long story. I suggest that after we have rounded up these villains, we repair to a little drinking establishment I know, where we can exchange information.'

'I could certainly do with a drink.'

'We've got Petters and Foy and most of the gang,' said a uniformed officer breaking into the conversation.

'Good work Captain. We will be interested in what they have got to say for themselves back at the station. Where's O'Callaghan?'

'I'm afraid he has gone, Mr Richardson.'

'What do you mean "gone"?' snapped the Pinkerton agent.

'He must have slipped out unnoticed in the dark, down the back stairway. I've sent two of my men after him. Hopefully they will soon apprehend the felon.'

'Dash it! I shouldn't be so sure of that. O'Callaghan is a slippery character. I've been after him for years.'

'Sorry, Mr Richardson,' muttered the officer.

'Well, there's nothing else for it. We will be along later to the station to see what we can get out of these villains, after I have given poor Inspector Ravenscroft here some liquid refreshment. I don't know, you English are always getting yourselves in trouble, and expecting us Americans to come to your assistance,' joked Richardson. 'I wonder how many more times we will have to do that in the years ahead?'

* * *

'Here, take a swig of that,' said Richardson placing a glass before Ravenscroft.

'What is it?'

'Bourbon. It comes all the way from Kentucky, the finest American whisky.'

Ravenscroft picked up the glass and swallowed some of its contents. 'It is certainly strong.'

'It can't be beaten.'

'Indeed. It seems, Mr Richardson, that I owe you a deep debt of gratitude for saving my life.'

'Think nothing of it,' replied the Pinkerton man, replenishing Ravenscroft's glass from the bottle on the table.

'I believe you may also have been instrumental in saving my wife from those criminals in Limehouse.'

'All part of the job.'

'If you had not rescued Lucy, I am sure she would have been taken captive to one of their opium dens. It does not bear thinking about.'

'Always like to rescue a damsel in distress,' smiled Richardson before downing another glass.

'I believe it would be most beneficial to both of us if we shared our knowledge of this case,' suggested Ravenscroft.

'My very thoughts; you have heard of Pinkerton's?'

'Of course; America's leading detective agency.'

'We sure are. Our motto is "The eye never sleeps." Once we have a man in our sights we won't rest until he is brought to justice. Do you know there are more Pinkerton agents in the States now than there are members of the US Army?' boasted Richardson.

'There must be a great deal of crime over here.'

'There sure is!'

'Tell me all that you know about O'Callaghan.'

'He is one of the greatest villains ever to have walked this planet. The Pinkertons have been after him for at least ten years now, but every time we have come close to apprehending him the man slips though our fingers. Petters and Foy are his main associates, but there are many others in the criminal fraternity. Their speciality is breaking into banks. Foy is an expert safe blower, whereas it is Petters who is the strongman of the outfit. O'Callaghan is the brains, of course; he plans each robbery meticulously. They started out by raiding banks here in New York, but when things got too hot for them they went to other parts of America. There was a big job in Frisco three years back; before that there was one in New

Orleans, and all the time O'Callaghan has been getting richer and richer. He lives in a fine house in Boston. They are pretty audacious as well. On their last job here they even dug a tunnel from a nearby building right into the vaults of the bank.'

'A bit like the Red-Headed League,' interjected Ravenscroft.

'Red-Headed League?' Richardson looked puzzled.

'Sorry, it's a story by a British writer, Mr Arthur Conan Doyle. But if you know all this about O'Callaghan, why have you never been able to arrest him?' asked Ravenscroft.

'Because unfortunately he has a great many members of the police authorities in his pocket, and he also employs a very smart lawyer. Anyway, to resume, two years ago we learned that O'Callaghan had moved his activities across to your country.'

'Go on.'

'Last year there was a big robbery at one of the jewellers in Bond Street in London. They got away with some very choice items, by all accounts.'

'Yes I remember reading about it at the time. No one was caught.'

'Exactly. Then there was a bank robbery in Birmingham. Foy blew the safe. We believe they got away with a great deal of money and bonds that time, although the bank's people were not exactly forthcoming in regard to the true amount. They had their reputation to uphold.'

'That is understandable. Now tell me where Mr Rockstone fits into all this?' asked Ravenscroft.

'Silas Rockstone is a complete charlatan and thief.'

'And is he an associate of O'Callaghan?'

'Oh yes. They go back together a long way. They were involved in the civil war together, although we cannot be sure which side they supported, the Unionists or the Confederates, as they were often in the habit of faking their own deaths and selling armaments to both sides. They were as thick as two thieves. Why they even courted the same woman, the infamous Kitty O'Mara, mistress of the Kentucky Casino.'

'So what was Rockstone doing in England?'

'We know that he left New York just over a year ago. Things were getting rather hot for him over here, and I guess he just wanted to go somewhere different until things had cooled down, or so we thought, but of course he was an important part of O'Callaghan's operation in England. Have another drink?'

'No thank you,' replied Ravenscroft, feeling that the liquor was beginning to have its effect on him.

'We believe that Rockstone committed a number of robberies in your country during the past year. He uses the travelling fair as his cover. As it moves around the country Rockstone seeks out likely places to burgle — usually empty houses when the people are away — small country banks with obsolete safes — that sort of thing. We believe that he was stashing away the spoils then passing them on later to his old friend O'Callaghan.'

'So the valuables he stole would eventually find their way to New York?'

'Precisely. If Rockstone tries to pawn or sell the stolen items in England, there would be a chance that they would be identified and traced back to him, but of course in New York the valuables could be sold without any fear of that happening.'

'Very clever, but tell me where did the murdered man Jacob fit into all this?'

Richardson sat back in his chair and smiled. 'Jacob Kelly was a petty crook who joined up with Rockstone a couple of years ago before they went to England. What Rockstone did not know, of course, was that Jacob was our man.'

'You mean that Jacob was a Pinkerton agent?' asked Ravenscroft, surprised.

'Not exactly. Two years ago, Jacob had got himself into a lot of trouble here in New York, stealing from one or two high-class establishments. We caught him in the act, as they say, and we saw a wonderful opportunity opening up for us. We did a deal with Jacob: he would not go to prison, and in exchange he would work for us. We needed someone on the inside. So we suggested that he get friendly with Rockstone and become his accomplice. In time we hoped that he would lead us O'Callaghan himself.'

'I see. And was that why you were in England when Jacob was killed?'

'We had heard nothing from Jacob since he had arrived in your country, but we knew something big was probably about to take place. The agency decided to send me over there, to find out what had happened to Jacob. Unfortunately I arrived three days too late in Ledbury. He was already dead by then.'

'So you think Rockstone found out that Jacob was working for the Pinkertons, and that is why he was killed?'

'It seems highly likely.'

'Why did you take the photographs of Jacob, and also destroy the negatives?'

'Jacob had been involved in a small way in a number of Pinkerton investigations, some of them on-going. We did not want to run the risk that someone would come forward and claim to have recognised him; that might give other villains the idea that we were on to them. I learned that you were investigating the case, and that your wife was travelling to London to collect some information for you, so that was why I decided to follow her that day.'

'It was fortunate that you did so.'

'What I could not understand, Inspector Ravenscroft, is why your wife visited the Foundling Hospital, and then Mincing and Stricket?'

'I think it is time I told you of the developments in this case you haven't been able to piece together yourself.'

'If you would, I would be most obliged.'

During the next few minutes Ravenscroft recounted how he and Constable Crabb had recovered the locket from Rockstone, and of its miniature inside, and how this had led him to the artist Louis Thermaine in Cirencester, and then to Maria Constantine at the Verzons, and how Lucy had learned the woman's tragic story which in turn had taken her to London and him to New York.'

'So you think that Thomas Temple was the true name of our fellow, Jacob Kelly?' asked Richardson after he had listened intently to Ravenscroft's account.

'I don't honestly know if I can answer that question. Temple supposedly left Macy's store in 1885 in order to return to England, but of course he may have remained in New York and changed his name to Jacob. Can you tell me anything about Jacob before you arrested him two years ago?'

'I am afraid I cannot help you much there. Jacob was involved in criminal activities in New York for at least a year before we arrested him in 1889. Beyond that, we have no record of him.'

'So if he did go to England in 1885, he could well have returned to New York sometime before 1888?'

'That could be likely. I am sorry I cannot help you further.'

'One more question.'

'Only one?' smiled Richardson.

'What were O'Callaghan and his associates doing on the *Etruria*? And why were you on the same ship? Although I think I know the answer to the second question.'

'As I said earlier, I was aware of your involvement in the case, and at that time believed that if I followed you, you might just provide me with the answers I was looking for. I was surprised to see that O'Callaghan, Petters and Foy, were also on board. I believe they were returning to their homeland because they considered it safe to do so, now that Jacob was dead.'

'They could have met up with Rockstone before they left England?'

'Who, no doubt, passed over some of the valuables he had stolen, although it is my belief that O'Callaghan would not have been so foolish as to actually have stolen goods in his possession. He could not run the risk of being apprehended by the authorities upon his return to New York. No, the jewels and other valuables were being transported from your country to New York through Mincing and Stricket. I believe we have netted quite a haul tonight in that warehouse.'

'It would have been the perfect cover. It would also explain why Thomas Temple was arrested for receiving stolen goods. The gang could have been using Mincing and Stricket for years to transport stolen valuables under cover to New York.'

'Could well have done. And now, it is time we visited the police station and see what we can get out of those villains, Petters and Foy. Would you care to accompany me, Inspector?'

Ravenscroft rose from his chair and followed the Pinkerton agent out of the room. Now at last he realised that the captured criminals might be able to provide him with the information he so desperately sought about Jacob's murder, and the reasons why he had been killed.

* * *

'Now then, Petters, you will no doubt be aware that your boss O'Callaghan has left you and your companions to accept all the blame,' said Richardson as he and Ravenscroft faced the criminal across the table in the dimly lit police room.

'I don't know what you are talking about,' muttered Petters.

The Pinkerton agent read from a sheet of paper in front of him. 'Twenty cardboard boxes found in the warehouse, containing numerous pieces of jewellery and other precious items, stolen from households in England, and shipped across here by the London merchants Mincing and Stricket.'

'I don't know what you are talking about,' repeated Petters arrogantly as he leaned back in his chair and drummed his fingers on the table.

'My colleague here saw you remove one of the parcels from the warehouse earlier today. You are in a great deal of trouble, Petters — receiving and dealing in stolen goods, threatening to kill a police officer, burglary and theft — the list is endless. You are going to prison for a very long time. There is a rather draughty, uncomfortable cell on Blackwell's Island which has been reserved for you, and while you are there for the next fifteen years you can remember that your boss O'Callaghan will be living the high life in his nice cosy mansion in Boston. That does not sound quite right to me, does it, letting you and Foy take all the blame while he goes completely free?'

'So what? I don't give a damn.'

'You tell us what you know, and in return we might have a word with the authorities to see that you receive a lighter sentence,' said Richardson. 'That cell over at Blackwell's Penitentiary can be mighty cold and uncomfortable at this time of the year. Fifteen years? I don't reckon you'll last beyond three, unless you go mad before then.'

Beneath Petters' bravado, Ravenscroft could see their quarry had a look of fear in his eyes.

'Tell me what you want to know,' said Petters after a long silence.

'Firstly, I want to know where O'Callaghan might be hiding. You know all his old haunts. He must be somewhere here in New York?'

'No, I can't do that. If ever he found out that I had told you that, my life would be gone.'

'Who committed the Bond Street robbery in London, then?' said Richardson, looking down at his paper again.

'Yes, that was me.'

'Who was with you?'

'Foy and O'Callaghan.'

'What about the bank robbery in Birmingham?'

'Yes, that was me as well,' sighed Petters.

'Now we are getting somewhere. I take it you were also involved in the bank robberies in Frisco and New Orleans?' continued Richardson, pressing home his advantage.

'Yes,' muttered Petters in an almost inaudible whisper.

'I am sorry, Mr Petters, my colleague here did not hear you.'

'Yes, yes,' replied the criminal irritably.

'When did you and O'Callaghan and Foy travel over to England?'

'I cannot remember.'

'Try. We can check the passenger lists.'

'Six months ago.'

'What was the purpose of your visit there?'

'I would rather not say.'

'Come now, Petters, this will not do, just when things were going well for you. I will ask you one more time — why did you go to England?'

'Things were getting hot for us here, after the Manhattan diamond break-in.'

'I *thought* O'Callaghan was behind that,' said Richardson with a degree of satisfaction.

'So we decided to lie low in England until things quietened down.'

'Did you see Mr Rockstone while you were in England?' interjected Ravenscroft.

'We met up with him in London. He told us he had arranged for the valuables to be parcelled up and sent over to the warehouse here by Mincing and Stricket.'

'Was Jacob Kelly with Rockstone?'

'Who's Jacob Kelly?' replied Petters with a look of puzzlement on his face.

Annoyed, Richardson raised his voice. 'Oh come now, Petters, you know who Jacob was.'

'Alright, alright. I had met him once or twice in New York, two or three years ago.'

'That's better. Now, was Jacob with Rockstone when you met him in London?' continued the Pinkerton detective.

'No.'

'But you knew that Jacob was working with Rockstone?' Ravenscroft leaned forwards and looked Petters directly in the eyes.

'I had heard something about that.'

'You know that Jacob is dead?'

'No.'

'We found him hanged from a tree, on a desolate hill near Malvern.'

'I didn't have anything to do with it,' protested Petters, showing a look of alarm.

'So you knew that Jacob had been killed?'

'No, not until you mentioned it just now.'

'Did Rockstone ask you to travel to Ledbury, and take Jacob there, and hang him from a tree?'

'No. What is this? Where is this Ledbury, and this Malvern? I've never been to such places. I don't know what you are talking about,' pleaded Petters anxiously.

'Come on, Petters,' interrupted Richardson. 'If you didn't kill poor Jacob, then you know who did. Was it Foy who killed him, or O'Callaghan, or Rockstone himself?'

'I tell you, Mr Richardson, I don't know what you are talking about. I hardly knew this Jacob. I certainly never met him while we were in England. I will confess to all the robberies but I never committed any murder. You know murder is not my thing. I would never hurt a fly. You must believe me,' implored Petters.

Ravenscroft looked at Richardson, who nodded in his direction.

'Take him away, officer,' said the Pinkerton man after a moment's silence had passed.

'I tell you, I know nothing about this murder. We were just in London looking at one or two jobs for the future,' said Petters as he was led away. 'You cannot hang it on me.'

'You believe him, Inspector Ravenscroft?' asked Richardson after the door had closed.

'Strangely, I do. I don't think O'Callaghan or his associates did kill Jacob.'

'I am inclined to agree with you. Murder is not one of O'Callaghan's usual crimes, although I must admit that he was going to make an exception concerning you. Rockstone must still be your most likely candidate?'

'Yes, that is why I need to return home as soon as possible. I want to secure the arrest of Silas Rockstone, and equally as important, I want to find out what happened to Thomas Temple after he left Macy's,' said Ravenscroft.

'Then we had better secure you a return berth on the next ship out of New York. I am sorry that we have not been able to assist you in your search. It's been a pleasure meeting you, Inspector Ravenscroft.'

'And you, Agent Richardson. Oh, there is one more thing that you can do for me before I leave.'

'Just ask.'

'Do you know of anyone who sells butterflies?'

CHAPTER TWELVE

HEREFORDSHIRE

'Well, Mrs Ravenscroft, that was certainly a clever idea of yours to go back to the Reading Rooms in Malvern, if I may so,' said Crabb as the trap made its way out towards the Verzons.

'I just knew that it might prove worthwhile to see what else had been written in the local paper concerning the death of Lizzie Warren,' replied Lucy. 'I wonder why Francis Constantine attended poor Lizzie's funeral.'

'Perhaps it was Mr Constantine who met Lizzie Warren on the hill that day?' suggested Crabb.

'You think he could have caused her death?'

'I don't know, Mrs Ravenscroft, but it will certainly be interesting to hear what he has to say about the matter.'

Crabb turned the trap into the courtyard of the Verzons, where they were met by the loud barking of a sheepdog.

'I think it might be better if we remained in the trap until someone comes,' said Lucy.

'That animal certainly does not appear to want us here,' replied Crabb, keeping a tight hold on the reins as the startled horse refused to stay still.

'Here, Brutus! Down!' came a man's shout.

The dog dropped to the floor and remained stationary.

'Oh, it is you again, Constable Crabb. I wondered who had frightened him,' said Francis Constantine, emerging from one of the barns at the same moment that his sister appeared from the house. 'No Inspector Ravenscroft this time?'

'He's away on business, sir,' answered Crabb, helping Lucy to step out of the trap. 'May I introduce Mrs Ravenscroft.'

'Mrs Ravenscroft,' nodded Constantine.

'I am pleased to make your acquaintance, Mr Constantine, and Miss Constantine,' said Lucy.

'Well, Crabb, what have you come here for?' asked Constantine bluntly. 'I thought we had told you all about my sister's locket the last time you called.'

Maria spoke up. 'Mrs Ravenscroft, perhaps you would like to come indoors and take some refreshment with me while my brother talks with the constable.'

'That would be most kind of you, Miss Constantine,' said Lucy, and followed Maria into the house.

'Now then, Crabb, what is all this about?' asked Francis Constantine. 'I have not a great deal of time to indulge in idle chatter. I'm on the way to feed some of the sheep, so you will have to walk with me into the fields.'

'Thank you, sir; I will not take up too much of your time.'

* * *

'Quickly, we may not have much time.' Maria closed the door. 'My brother must not know that we have met before today.'

'Of course, I understand.'

'You have news of my son?'

'I am afraid not. My husband has gone to America, as I communicated to you in my letter. He should have arrived

155

in New York several days ago. I am sure that if your son is still in New York my husband will find him.'

'It is so strange that he left his employment without a word to his employers all those years ago. I wonder why?' asked an anxious Maria.

'Perhaps he was offered a better position. I am sure that my husband will return soon, and any news that he has obtained I will pass on to you by letter as soon as possible,' said Lucy trying to sound as reassuring as she could.

'I do hope your husband is able to find my son. I could not bear to grow old without knowing what had happened to him,' said Maria, tears beginning to form in her eyes.

'I am sure all will be well. You must have courage to wait a while longer.'

'I have already waited for over thirty years. It is imperative that my brother never finds out what happened all those years ago.'

'I understand. Maria, I want to ask you a question. Do you recall a woman by the name of Lizzie Warren?'

'Lizzie Warren? The name seems familiar. What has she to do with my son?'

'Lizzie Warren died in unfortunate circumstances on Hangman Hill nearly ten years ago,' replied Lucy, ignoring the question. 'She died as the result of a fall.'

'What a terrible thing to have happened. Yes, I do remember reading about the unfortunate incident in the newspaper at the time.'

'I have just been reading the newspaper report of her funeral, which was held at Little Malvern Priory. Your brother was listed as one of the mourners. Can you think of any reason why he would have attended the internment?'

'I do not know. You must ask him.'

'I think Constable Crabb may be asking your brother the same question.'

'Yes, of course. I remember now. How silly of me to forget, but it was all such a long time ago. Francis was Lizzie Warren's godfather.'

'So your brother knew the family?'

'Yes, he must have done. It was all such a long time ago. I think my brother knew Stephen Warren. He was a tenant farmer near Eastnor. When Lizzie was born Mr Warren asked Francis if he would be godfather to his daughter Lizzie. I remember Francis saying at the time that he hardly knew the man, but he felt that he could not refuse such a personal request.'

'I noticed that there were no Warrens recorded at the funeral service.'

'Yes that would be correct. Warren's wife died when Lizzie was little more than an infant, and Stephen Warren died a few years later. There were no other children, I believe. It was quite a sad case. The farm was rented out to another family. I do not know what happened to Lizzie after that.'

'She gained employment with a Mr Rostagon, a farmer out at Parkway.'

'I see. I suppose my brother must have read about her death, and decided to pay his respects at her funeral, as her godfather. But I don't know why you want to know all this? How is all this relevant to the search for my son?'

'We think that the man murdered on Hangman Hill may have met Lizzie on the morning she was killed. They were possibly romantically attached.'

'I see. I think my brother and your colleague are returning. We must go back to them.'

'Yes. Thank you for your information relating to your brother and Lizzie Warren.'

'Please, as soon as you know something . . .' Her voice trailed off to a whisper as she opened the door into the yard.

'You can trust me, Miss Constantine.'

'Ah, there you are,' said Francis Constantine.

'Have you told Constable Crabb everything you know?' Maria smiled.

'Nothing much to tell,' replied the landowner.

'Well Miss Constantine, it has been a pleasure to meet you,' said Lucy before climbing into the trap.

The brother and sister watched as the trap made its way out of the stable yard and on to the road.

* * *

On the journey back to Ledbury, Lucy related all that had taken place inside the Verzons.

'So Francis Constantine was Lizzie Warren's godfather!' exclaimed Crabb.

'Why are you so surprised, Tom? Did he not admit the same to you?' asked Lucy.

'No. He said he had never heard of her, and that the newspaper report of him attending the funeral must have been erroneous.'

'I wonder why Francis did not offer to take the child under his care and protection when her parents died. It could not have been an easy life working at Mr Rostagon's farm. I have no reason however to doubt that Maria Constantine was telling me the truth.'

'If that is so, Mrs Ravenscroft, why did Francis Constantine deny ever having known Lizzie Warren? Why did he not just tell me the truth? What is he hiding?'

* * *

Two days later Constable Crabb and Sergeant Morris were mingling with the crowds at the autumn fair in the busy Herefordshire market town of Ross-on-Wye. Both men had relinquished their police uniforms and were attired in clothes that were more suited to farm labourers.

'Well, Constable Crabb, have you caught sight of this American Rockstone yet?' asked the older man.

'No, Sergeant. I recognise Mr Walker over there, trying to separate those poor lads from their hard-earned wages. He is the owner of the fair. I am sure that Rockstone must be here somewhere.' Crabb pulled down his cap so that his features were hidden from view.

'Perhaps he will not come back to the fair now that it has returned to Herefordshire,' suggested Morris. 'He must know that the police are still on the lookout for him.'

'I fear that I may have called you out on a worthless errand,' sighed Crabb, frustrated.

'Never mind lad. We will give it a few more minutes before we call off the search.'

'Quickly, move over here, Sergeant!' said Crabb suddenly, indicating that Morris should join him behind one of the stalls.

'You have seen him?'

'No, but I know that youth over there, the one wearing the blue trousers and a green hat pulled down over his face. He was part of Rockstone's sales pitch: he was the stooge in the crowd who professed to have undertaken Rockstone's miracle cure,' whispered Crabb.

'Well spotted, Constable.'

'I suggest we follow him. He may lead us to Rockstone.'

'Good thinking.'

As the youth moved away from crowd and made his way down the main street of the town, Crabb and Morris followed on discreetly behind.

'He is turning down that road at the bottom of the hill,' said Crabb.

'Better give him a few seconds, we don't want to frighten him,' cautioned Morris.

'Perhaps he is meeting up with Rockstone and they are going to break into one of the houses,' suggested Crabb.

After some moments had passed, the two men turned the corner and were relieved to see the youth walking under the gas lamps in the distance.

'He may be leaving town,' said Morris, quickening his pace.

'Wait!' indicated Crabb. 'Look, he is meeting someone at the end of the road.'

'Is it your man Rockstone?'

'I cannot see his features, it is so dark.'

159

'They appear to be conversing together.'

'They have now gone across to that house. There appears to be no one at home, as the house is in darkness,' said Crabb.

'I suppose the owners and the servants have all gone to the fair. Keep back, Constable Crabb! We must not be seen,' urged Morris. 'You were right, lad. They appear to be forcing open one of the front windows.'

The two policemen watched as the youth and his associate climbed in through the window and disappeared from view.

'Now we shall have them,' said Morris.

'What shall we do, Sergeant?' asked Crabb.

'Wait here until they come out. We will catch them red-handed. No point following them inside. We would have difficulty seeing our way from one room to another in the dark,' answered Morris.

'They could leave by another exit?' suggested Crabb.

'Good thinking, Constable. You remain here. I will make my way down the road and round to the back of the houses. If they come out before I return, blow your whistle, draw your truncheon and then arrest them.'

'Right, Sergeant.'

'On no account move away from here unless you hear my whistle. Is that understood?'

'Yes, Sergeant.'

'I will be back before you know it.' Morris gave a friendly wink.

Crabb watched as his superior walked briskly past the group of terraced houses and then disappeared from view.

As his eyes focused on the window where the men had just entered, Crabb's thoughts turned to the many previous occasions when he and Ravenscroft had found themselves in similar situations, watching and waiting for criminals to appear, and he could not help but recall those unfortunate times when things had gone wrong and their adversary had absconded before they had secured an arrest. There had been successes and failures over the years, but now he was determined that this would be one occasion when his opponent would not escape police custody. If the mystery of Jacob's death was to be solved, then Rockstone must be apprehended at all costs.

The wait seemed endless. Perhaps Rockstone's accomplice had observed the policemen on his tail? If so, then the criminals might well have decided to leave from the back of the property. If that was the case, then surely they would have encountered his colleague? But if they had done so, they could have attacked the policeman and rendered him unconscious before he had been able to raise the alarm. Morris had certainly been gone for a long time, and Crabb became increasingly uneasy that his colleague had not returned. His heart pounded and sweat ran down his back. His inclination was to follow in the footsteps of the older policeman, and see whether he had been injured, but Morris had been adamant that he was not to leave his station on any account, and that he was to remain vigilant and prepared for any eventuality.

Suddenly he saw an indistinct movement inside the room, and then the window gradually swung open. Crabb removed his truncheon and whistle from the inside pocket of his coat. First the youth, then his accomplice stepped over the window ledge and into the road, the former carrying what appeared to be a large sack over his shoulder.

Raising his whistle to his lips, Crabb let out three loud blasts before running across the road towards the two startled men.

'Quick, it's the law!' shouted the youth dropping the bag on the pavement.

'Stay where you are!' Crabb, brandished his truncheon as he neared the two men. 'It is the police! There is no escape, raise your hands!'

'Alright, my friend,' replied the older man, complying with the request.

'Rockstone!' exclaimed Crabb drawing nearer.

'Grab him, boss! There are two of us and only one of him,' shouted the youth, approaching Crabb in a menacing manner.

'I warn you, give yourselves up. There are more of us than you can see.' Crabb tried to sound as bold as he could.

'Oh, I think you are bluffing, my friend,' laughed Rockstone.

'Come on, boss!' The youth ran head-first into Crabb, winding the policeman and knocking him to the ground.

'Grab his truncheon,' shouted Rockstone as Crabb and his adversary wrestled on the cobble stones.

'I'll take out his eyes!' replied the youth, wrenching the truncheon from Crabb's hand, but almost instantly dropping it in the tussle.

'I've got it,' shouted Rockstone picking up the weapon.

'Hit him with it, boss,' yelled the youth.

As Crabb looked up he could see Rockstone raising the truncheon above him.

'I would not do that, if I were you,' interjected a familiar voice.

Morris bought his truncheon forcefully across the man's legs. Rockstone dropped the weapon and let out a cry of pain. Crabb gained the upper hand on his opponent and pinned him to the ground, as Rockstone writhed in agony on the pavement.

'Put the cuffs on him, Constable Crabb,' said Morris.

Crabb reached into his pocket, withdrew the cuffs and secured them round the youth's wrists.

'Now then Mr Rockstone, are you going to come quietly, or would you like another dose of my truncheon?' asked Morris, standing over the outstretched American.

'Confound you!' Rockstone slowly staggered to his feet, rubbing his leg.

Morris seized the showman's hands and clasped a pair of cuffs round his wrists.

'Thank you, Sergeant,' said Crabb, pulling the defeated youth to his feet.

'All in a day's work, Constable Crabb,' smiled Morris.

'You cannot arrest me, my man,' said Rockstone. 'I am a citizen of the Americas.'

'I don't care if you are the President of the United States, or the Archangel Gabriel, you and your friend here are coming along with us,' said Morris taking hold of his captive's arm.

'I know you,' said Rockstone staring at Crabb. 'You were at the fair in Ledbury, with that Inspector Ravenscroft.'

'That is correct. We have been after you for a very long time; a very long time indeed,' said Crabb.

CHAPTER THIRTEEN

AT SEA

Ravenscroft stood on the promenade deck of the *Etruria* looking down on the remaining passengers, who were eagerly making their way along the dockside and up on to the gangplank of the vessel that would shortly be departing on its transatlantic return trip to England. Many of his sailing companions were already waving handkerchiefs and flags at their loved ones gathered along the harbourside. A six-piece band was busily engaged in playing American melodies, as a number of porters carrying cases and trunks of all shapes and colours struggled to make their way on board the ship.

Ravenscroft reflected on the days he had spent in the great city, and the journey he had undertaken from the grimy interior of Ma Scrivens' Lodging House in Manhattan, to the forlorn prison on Blackwell's Island and the opulence and splendour of Macy's Department Store in central New York, to the desperate situation he had found himself in at the near deserted warehouse of Mincing and Stricket, and of his rescue by Richardson the Pinkerton agent. Now as he stood looking out at the busy scene, he could not help but feel a little sad that the adventure was almost over, as well as being somewhat disappointed that despite all his efforts he had still not discovered the fate of Maria Constantine's missing son. To add to his frustration was the fact that he was also no further forward in discovering who had murdered Jacob Kelly, and whether the dead man had once been Thomas Temple or whether they had been two different men. Perhaps a few days' quiet contemplation at sea would provide him with the opportunity to reflect on past events, and help him to see how he could proceed with the case when he returned home.

He was awakened rudely from his deliberations by a loud blast from the ship, indicating that its departure was imminent.

'Ravenscroft! Ravenscroft!' shouted a familiar voice.

He strained to see the speaker amongst the waving crowds.

'Ravenscroft!' shouted the voice again.

'Here!' replied the detective recognising Bill Richardson the Pinkerton agent, who was frantically engaged in waving a white envelope above his head. Ravenscroft pushed his way quickly along the crowded deck full of passengers as he made his way towards the gangplank.

'All aboard! Last call!' shouted a seaman about to haul up the wooden staircase.

'Wait!' cried Ravenscroft. 'I must see that man. He has something for me.'

'No one else is allowed ashore.'

'But it is imperative, I see him. It is important police business.'

'Sorry, sir, but—'

'Ravenscroft!' Richardson was already running up the gangway.

Ravenscroft brushed past the seaman and raced down to join Richardson.

'Here, take this!' The Pinkerton agent thrust the envelope into Ravenscroft's hand.

'Have you caught O'Callaghan yet?'

'No, but it will only be a matter of time. Have a good voyage.'

'All aboard!' yelled out the seaman.

'Thank you for everything,' shouted Ravenscroft, quickly retracing his steps as the wooden planks moved beneath his feet.

'See you in Herefordshire someday,' laughed the Pinkerton agent as he made his way back on to dry land.

Ravenscroft walked along the deck, eventually finding a place near the rail between the waving and cheering passengers, as the ship gave out another blast from its funnel. He looked out at the crowd on the harbour side, and saw Richardson giving a brief wave in his direction, before the Pinkerton agent disappeared in a sea of waving hands and flags.

As the ship pulled away from the harbour wall, and the cheering crowds began to recede slowly into the distance, Ravenscroft looked out across the sea towards the large impressive statue brandishing its torch of liberty and hope, jutting out into the waters, and which seemed to him to be like some guardian and protector of its country, before making his way down towards his cabin.

* * *

Ravenscroft studied once more the three items on the bed before him, which he had removed from Richardson's envelope.

The first had been a hastily scribbled note from the Pinkerton man. 'I have just discovered that your man Temple shared a cell with Jacob during their time in Blackwell's!'

The second was a copy of a Passenger List dated 7 September 1885, for a ship leaving New York for England, which included the name Thomas Temple.

The third, Ravenscroft recognised. It was the photograph of the dead man Jacob, which Richardson had previously removed from his office in Ledbury.

So now he knew that Thomas Temple and Jacob Kelly were two different men!

The man found hanging on Hangman Hill had been the New York petty criminal and informant, and not Maria Constantine's son. Temple and Jacob had evidently shared a cell together on the prison island all those years ago. Was that how Jacob had acquired Temple's locket? Had he stolen it from his companion one night when he had been asleep, or even taken it from him by force? He could not imagine that Temple would have given away his most prized possession.

Then there was the passenger list, which proved that when Temple had left Macy's he had indeed returned to England. But that had been six years ago. What had happened to Temple when the ship had docked in Liverpool? He had been able to trace Temple's movements during his time in America, but now Ravenscroft was faced with an even greater problem: to discover what had happened to Temple when he had returned to England. The more he thought about it, the more he came to the sad conclusion that his quest might go unresolved. At least he would be able to tell Maria Constantine that the dead man on Hangman Hill had not been her son.

It was fortunate that he now had the photograph of the dead Jacob, so that he could continue his enquiries when he returned to Ledbury, and there was always the hope that Crabb might have caught up with Rockstone during his absence, and that the murder would have been solved.

After dressing for dinner, Ravenscroft made his way to the second-class dining room, where he told the waiter that he wished to dine alone. He had no inclination to be sociable that night, and after his experience on the outward journey, had no desire to be seated with another group of strangers.

Allocated a corner seat, Ravenscroft spent the next hour eating, reading, and gazing out of the window at the people walking up and down on the deck.

He suddenly caught sight of a familiar figure, dressed in a long dark astrakhan overcoat, passing swiftly by on the deck.

'Good God! It's O'Callaghan!' he exclaimed, rising from his seat quickly, and nearly colliding with a waiter as he did so.

Ravenscroft ran across the dining room, much to the alarm of both diners and waiters, and out through the double doors on to the deck. He looked frantically for the figure, but could see no one. Had O'Callaghan seen him and made his escape?

Ravenscroft ran along the deck, but there was no sign of the man. As he turned the corner of the promenade deck, and found himself on the other side of the ship, he saw a familiar figure in the distance, tall and grey-haired, and ran quickly towards him.

'So, O'Callaghan, we have caught you at last!' exclaimed Ravenscroft grabbing the man's shoulder.

'I beg your pardon!' exclaimed the other indignantly. Certainly this fellow was the same age as O'Callaghan, and dressed in a similar astrakhan overcoat and fur hat, but their faces were completely different.

'Forgive me. I am so sorry. I mistook you for someone else,' stuttered Ravenscroft embarrassed.

The man gave him a stern look of reproach before continuing his walk around the deck.

Ravenscroft let out a deep sigh, removed his spectacles and wiped them on his handkerchief. Had he really seen O'Callaghan, or had his memory played tricks on him? Surely the criminal would not have dared to escape his captors in New York by securing a berth on the same ship that had recently brought him to America?

During the next thirty minutes Ravenscroft walked the many decks of the ship desperately searching for the criminal in all the public rooms and corridors, but without success. Finally he made his way to the office in the centre of the ship.

'Good evening to you, sir; how may I be of assistance?' asked the young polite receptionist standing behind a counter.

'I wonder if I might look at the passenger list?' replied Ravenscroft.

'I am sorry, sir, but that is not possible.'

'Oh, why is that?'

'The company insists on the confidentiality of all its passengers.'

'I am a police officer, and I believe that one of your passengers may be a wanted criminal.'

'Really, sir? If you would care to wait here for a moment,' said the receptionist, before going over towards his older companion who had been busily writing further along the counter.

Ravenscroft shuffled uneasily as he watched the two men whispering intently together.

'I understand that you wish to see the passenger list, sir?' asked the second, more senior receptionist, looking intently at Ravenscroft.

'Yes. I am an English police officer. I have reason to believe that a Mr O'Callaghan might be on board. He is a notorious criminal wanted by the New York police,' said Ravenscroft, growing hot under his collar.

'As my colleague here has just informed you, I am afraid that will not be possible.'

Ravenscroft took out his identity card and placed it on the counter. 'The New York police and the Pinkerton Detective Agency are both searching for this man, and I also have reason to believe that he may have been responsible for a murder committed recently in England.'

The senior receptionist looked at Ravenscroft, then at his companion, and then again at Ravenscroft.

'I appreciate that you cannot let me see the passenger list, but at least could you check the register yourself?' pleaded Ravenscroft.

'I suppose it will do no harm.' The receptionist opened a large ledger that was on the counter. 'Callaghan, you said?'

'O'Callaghan,' corrected Ravenscroft.

The man ran his finger down the list of names. 'I am sorry, but there is no one with that name travelling on this ship.'

'I see. Then perhaps he is travelling under another name?'

'That could be possible, but maybe you were mistaken in regard to this possible passenger?' suggested the receptionist, adopting what Ravenscroft considered a superior manner.

'No, I am not mistaken.'

'Then I do not see how we can help you. All I can suggest, is that if you see this man again, you call for assistance, and we will apprehend the said gentleman.'

'Yes. Thank you for your assistance,' sighed Ravenscroft before walking away.

He was sure that it had been O'Callaghan that he had seen through the window, even if it had only been for a fraction of a second. It was obvious that the man was travelling under an assumed name. O'Callaghan was an experienced criminal. He would not have given his real name when he had embarked, knowing that the authorities in New York might still apprehend him, and if he had seen Ravenscroft through the dining-room window then that would have explained his sudden disappearance.

The *Etruria* had many cabins. Ravenscroft was sure that one of them contained the criminal mastermind, but he realised that neither he nor the ship's men, could search every one of them. He would just have to wait until O'Callaghan made another appearance.

* * *

During the next few days, as the *Etruria* made its way across the Atlantic Ocean towards the port of Liverpool, Ravenscroft walked the various decks of the vessel, seeking out the American, but achieved no success.

Now on the night before the ship's arrival, he stood alone on the promenade deck, looking out to sea, wondering what the next day would bring, and what news would be waiting for him upon his return to Ledbury. He could hear the distant sounds of voices shouting and singing to the accompaniment of a piano. A refreshing breeze blew across his face as he saw the distant light from a passing ship in the far distance.

He was disturbed by the opening of a door at the end of the deck. A white-coated steward emerged, head bent low, humming a tune as he began earnestly to mop the boards.

Ravenscroft took out his pocket watch, observed that the time was approaching eleven, and decided that he would shortly retire so that he would be up early the next day to watch the passengers leave the ship. He was determined that O'Callaghan would not escape. If the criminal did not disembark he resolved that he would call upon the Liverpool police to make a detailed search of the vessel.

Suddenly he felt a sharp pain in the side of his head, and his vision clouded over as he fell to the deck. He let out a loud groan and looked up to see a familiar face standing over him.

'O'Callaghan!' muttered Ravenscroft, as the American grabbed his arms and roughly hauled him upright.

'Damn you, Ravenscroft! Did you think you could arrest me?'

Ravenscroft could feel the blood pouring down his face, as his opponent pushed him up against the rails.

'You interfering fool!' growled O'Callaghan.

'Give yourself up, man. You won't get away with this.'

'Don't make me laugh, you stupid Englishman!' replied the American angrily.

'My companions will be waiting for me in Liverpool. If I am not there, they will search this ship until they find you,' blurted out Ravenscroft. His adversary appeared to be swaying from side to side in the darkness.

'You English, always useless when it comes to defeat,' snarled O'Callaghan as he began to push Ravenscroft backwards over the edge of the rail.

'No!' Ravenscroft lashed out with his foot, thrusting himself forwards, seeking to grab his opponent's arms.

'I'll have you, Ravenscroft!' shouted O'Callaghan as the two men grappled with one another.

Ravenscroft knew that he was fighting for his life. He momentarily saw Lucy in the mist that was beginning to close in upon him, and he made one last determined effort to break free from his adversary.

The two men separated.

'Curse you, Ravenscroft!' yelled O'Callaghan, rushing towards Ravenscroft again.

Ravenscroft threw himself to one side, as he felt the American rush past him. O'Callaghan let out a loud scream as he disappeared from view over the side of the ship. Ravenscroft dragged himself to his feet, and gazed at the waters below.

'Man overboard! Man overboard!' he shouted as he searched in the dark for any sign of O'Callaghan.

As he sought to support himself by holding on to the rail, he heard the sound of running feet and anxious shouting.

'He . . . he . . . tried to kill me,' he stuttered, grasping the lapel of an officer.

He heard a loud splash as someone threw a life jacket over the side.

'Bring a light!' instructed the officer. 'You there, take care of this man.'

Ravenscroft felt himself being supported by two men.

'It's no good. He's gone!' said another.

'Look again, I tell you!' shouted the officer. 'Shine that light down there.'

'There is nothing, sir.'

'Damn it!'

'Easy there,' said the officer to Ravenscroft. 'Take it easy. We will soon have you attended to.'

As Ravenscroft was taken below decks and his wound cleaned and dressed, he realised that he had been fortunate to have survived the attack. O'Callaghan was now dead, that was a fact, but with the criminal's demise might also have gone the last opportunity of knowing who had killed Jacob.

CHAPTER FOURTEEN

HEREFORDSHIRE

'You have a rather nasty bruise there,' said Lucy. 'Are you sure you would not like me to bathe it again for you?'

It was later the next day, and the detective, his wife and Crabb were sitting round the dining table in the small house in Church Lane in Ledbury, having each recounted their experiences during the past few weeks.

'There is no need. The ship's doctor attended to me after my encounter with O'Callaghan, and I felt much better this morning after a good night's sleep.'

'You had a lucky escape,' said Crabb sympathetically.

'Being nearly killed twice in seven days must be somewhat of a record even for you,' added Lucy light-heartedly.

'Yes. Do you know when that villain was about to throw me over the side, it was your face, Lucy, that suddenly appeared before me, and I think it was that which gave me the strength to not let him get the better of me. It is a pity that I was not able to question O'Callaghan. I am sure that he knew both Jacob Kelly and Thomas Temple, and that he was probably involved in the former's death.'

'Well at least you now know that Jacob Kelly and Thomas Temple were not the same man, and that Maria Constantine's son must still be alive,' said Lucy.

'We cannot be sure of that. All we know is that he returned to England sometime towards the end of 1885. Where he went to after that is anyone's guess.'

'At least it will be some consolation for Miss Constantine,' added Lucy. 'I will write to her later today.'

'So Jacob stole the locket while they were in prison?' asked Crabb.

'You would have thought he would have sold it at the first opportunity, instead of keeping it,' said Lucy.

'Yes, but he evidently took a liking to it and decided to keep it. It was fortunate for us that he did so, and that we compelled Rockstone to hand it over to us. Had he not done so, or had Jacob disposed of it earlier, we might not have been able to progress further with our investigations. It has been a long trail that has taken us from Cirencester, to the Verzons, to the Foundling Hospital and Mincing and Stricket in London, and across the Atlantic Ocean to New York, but it is still frustrating that after all that we are no further forward with discovering either who murdered Jacob, or where the elusive Thomas Temple is.'

'At least we have Rockstone and his accomplice in custody,' said Crabb.

'Indeed we have, and I must congratulate you, Tom, on an excellent piece of detective work during my absence. To realise that Rockstone was using the fair as cover for his criminal activities was clever, and you and Sergeant Morris did an excellent job in arresting the man. Have you been able to obtain any information from him?'

'His accomplice has admitted all the burglaries we knew about, and a few other ones as well, but Rockstone himself is denying everything, including the murder of Jacob Kelly,' replied Crabb.

'Perhaps now that we know that he was a former associate of O'Callaghan he might be more forthcoming with his answers. It seems that I must also thank you as well, my dear, for your uncovering of the death of Lizzie Warren. I should perhaps go away more often and leave the solving of crimes to you and Tom here,' Ravenscroft joked.

'I am pleased to assist you at any time,' laughed Lucy.

'From what you have told me, it seems that Lizzie Warren may have died as the result of some kind of an assault on Hangman Hill, rather than her death being caused by her falling and hitting her head on a rock. If that was the case then Jacob could have killed her. We know that she was seeing a man of that name at that time. They could have quarrelled, he pushed her, and she was killed. If that was the case, it seems we will never know the exact details of the incident, as both parties are now dead, but we do know that Jacob must have left for America shortly afterwards, and that when he returned to this country with Rockstone and learned that the fair was journeying to Hereford he was obviously very reluctant to travel there.'

'In case someone recognised him?' suggested Lucy.

'Exactly. And clearly someone did, for he was taken captive to Hangman Hill and strung up from one of the trees there, at exactly the same place where Lizzie Warren had been killed all those years before.'

'Someone was seeking revenge for Lizzie Warren's death,' interjected Crabb.

'Precisely, but who? You mentioned that Francis Constantine was Lizzie Warren's godfather?'

'But surely he would have not committed the crime?' Lucy said.

'He denied knowing Lizzie Warren when I questioned him,' Crabb reminded her.

'I know, but I still can't see him as the murderer.'

'Then there is this farmer, Rostagon,' went on Ravenscroft, 'the one who employed Lizzie. Perhaps he had been fond of her and wanted revenge on her assailant?'

'That could be a possibility. He certainly struck me as being rather an unpleasant man,' said Lucy.

'He was very abrupt, and seemed very uninterested in what we had to say,' added Crabb.

'And this young man working on the farm, the one who told you Jacob's name?'

'Michael Sangster,' said Crabb.

'Do you think he could have been romantically attached to Lizzie Warren?' asked Ravenscroft.

'It could have been the case, sir,' answered Crabb.

'So he could have been holding a grudge against Jacob for Lizzie's death, and years later when he saw Jacob at the fair in Hereford he decided to take the law into his own hands?'

'So we have Constantine, Rostagon and Sangster, any one of whom could have killed Jacob,' said Crabb.

'Or any combination of them. It may have taken two men to hang Jacob from that tree. However, we also have Rockstone as a possible suspect. He could have killed Jacob,' said Ravenscroft.

'But why?' asked Lucy.

'Because the two men had a falling out, or Jacob was threatening to expose Rockstone to the authorities,' suggested Ravenscroft.

'Yes, but if that was so, why take him out to Hangman Hill to end his life?' continued Lucy.

'To make us believe that Jacob's death was some kind of revenge killing. Jacob could have told Rockstone all about the events on the hill when Lizzie died, and Rockstone then saw how he could kill Jacob and make it look as though someone else had committed the crime. I think we are dealing with a very clever man. You say, Tom, that Rockstone is still in custody?'

'Yes, both he and his accomplice are at Hereford Police Station.'

'Then first thing tomorrow morning we will travel over to Hereford. Now that O'Callaghan is dead, Rockstone might be more inclined to confess his sins.'

* * *

176

'Good morning, Sergeant Morris,' said Ravenscroft as he and Crabb entered the police station in Hereford on the following morning.

'Good morning to you, Inspector,' replied the policeman, looking at the bruise on the side of Ravenscroft's head. 'It is good to see that you have returned . . . safely. How did you find New York, sir?'

'Fascinating and dangerous, but it seems that you and Constable Crabb have been especially busy during my absence?'

'Indeed we have. The villains are in the cells. The Rockstone fellow is saying nothing, but the other one, the young lad, has admitted everything.'

'Excellent. Perhaps you would be kind enough to bring Rockstone up to the interview room, Sergeant.'

'Certainly, sir.'

Ravenscroft and Crabb made their way to a grey, airless room at the back of the station.

'Now let us see what the American has to say for himself,' said Ravenscroft as he sat on a chair behind a small desk.

'You still think he killed Jacob?' asked Crabb.

'I don't know, but I mean to find out.'

The door opened and the handcuffed American and Sergeant Morris entered the room.

'Ah, Inspector Ravenscroft, I see,' smiled Rockstone.

'Take a seat, Mr Rockstone. I think we can dispense with the handcuffs, Sergeant Morris. I am confident that our prisoner won't be going anywhere for quite a long time, unless it is to the nearest prison.'

'You don't have anything on me, Inspector Ravenscroft,' laughed Rockstone as the policeman removed the cuffs.

'How would you explain your breaking and entering in Ross-on-Wye? And your attack on Constable Crabb here?'

'A misunderstanding, I can assure you,' replied Rockstone. He sat in the chair facing Ravenscroft.

'That is not what your accomplice has told us. He has confessed to everything, all the break-ins and robberies over the past few months. There was quite a long list of them. He will testify against you at your trial, no doubt in a futile attempt to save his own skin.'

'The boy is a fantasist. He knows nothing,' said Rockstone in a carefree manner.

'Is that so? I can assure you that we can match the dates of at least ten robberies with the places where the fair was situated. We know that as you went round the towns and villages putting up posters advertising the fair, you and your accomplice were on the lookout for suitable properties which you could later break into.'

'A mere coincidence, that is all I can say.'

'It would be in your interests to tell us where you have hidden all the items you appropriated.'

'I don't know what you are talking about. I am afraid that I cannot help you, Inspector, as I have not taken anything from anyone's house.' Rockstone leaned confidently back in his chair.

'Come now, Mr Rockstone, this will not do at all. We know that you and Jacob, and then you and the young lad we have in the cells, burgled all those houses. We also know that you then made up parcels of the stolen items, which you shipped to your associates in New York, using the services of Mincing and Stricket of Limehouse in London.'

'I am afraid I don't know what you are talking about. I have never heard of those people in London.'

'You may be interested to know, Mr Rockstone, that I have just returned from New York.'

'Is that where you acquired that bruise? New York can be a dangerous place for the unwary.'

'I was present when the police authorities and the Pinkerton agents raided Mincing and Stricket's warehouse in New York. We found some interesting parcels there. Furthermore, your associates O'Callaghan, Foy and Petters were also there.'

'I am sorry, I have never heard of these people,' said Rockstone, but his voice quivered. A slight chink had begun to appear in the suspect's armour.

'Foy and Petters are now in police custody in New York. They have told us everything concerning your activities in this country. They have provided us with quite a detailed account. I am afraid you will be in prison here for a very long time.'

'You have only their word for all this nonsense,' replied Rockstone defiantly.

'Your former associate O'Callaghan managed to escape. He then tried to throw me overboard on the return journey to England, but unfortunately for him, he lost his footing and fell into the sea. I have to tell you that O'Callaghan has now been consigned to the depths of the Atlantic Ocean. He will not be able to help you in the future.'

'How unfortunate for him,' said Rockstone. A brief smile crossed the American's face.

'So you see, Mr Rockstone, there is no way out. We have the confessions of Foy and Petters, and the young lad in the cells. I'm afraid it is all over for you.' Ravenscroft tried to sound as confident as he could.

'You cannot send me to prison. I am a citizen of the United States of America.'

'That's as may be, but that will not save you. I can assure you that there are many of your countrymen who have committed crimes in this country and who are now lingering in English prisons. They are all alone and face the prospect of never seeing either their homeland, or their loved ones ever again. Prison can be a very lonely, desperate place. Many of the prisoners never make it. Some go mad, others commit suicide, or die from maltreatment and disease, or are killed by other inmates.'

'Alright!' interrupted Rockstone banging his fist down hard on the table. 'You have made your point. You don't need to go on, man.'

'Then you admit to these crimes?' said Ravenscroft leaning forwards across the table.

Rockstone said nothing as he averted his eyes from Ravenscroft's stare.

'Then of course there is the matter of selling worthless pills and potions to innocent people . . .' continued Ravenscroft.

'My remedies bring great benefits.'

'However I am not really interested in all these burglaries and faked medicines. No, what really interests me is the death of your former assistant, Jacob.'

'I have told you all I know about Jacob.'

'Then you had better tell me it all over again,' emphasised Ravenscroft.

'I told you I met Jacob in New York. He was looking for work. I suggested he become my assistant. He accepted my offer. A few months later we came across to your country and joined Mr Walker's travelling fair,' sighed the American.

'And?'

'And what?'

'Why did you decide to kill him?'

'That is ridiculous. I had nothing to do with Jacob's demise. As I told you previously, Jacob was afraid to come back to Herefordshire.'

'Why was he afraid to return here?'

'I don't know. He never explained why.'

'I find that difficult to believe. Your colleague tells you that he does not wish to return to his home county, and you just accept what he says. You never thought to enquire further as to the reason?'

'No.'

'Well, I am afraid that I do not believe you. I think Jacob told you how he killed Lizzie Warren on Hangman Hill all those years ago, and that you saw it as the perfect opportunity to be rid of a man who you thought was about to betray you to the authorities,' said Ravenscroft forcibly.

'I am sorry, but this is all nonsense,' laughed Rockstone. 'Who is this Lizzie Warren? No doubt you will say that I killed her as well.'

'Lizzie Warren was an innocent young woman who was murdered on Hangman Hill some ten years ago.'

'I was in New York then.'

'Nevertheless, you killed Jacob. You hanged him from that tree on top of that hill.'

'Look Ravenscroft, this is all nonsense, utter nonsense. If I had wanted to kill Jacob, I would have buried him under six feet of earth, where you or anyone else would never have found him. I will take the blame for the robberies, but you sure as hell are not setting me up with a murder charge!' replied Rockstone, raising his voice.

'It is no use denying it, Rockstone. I believe you killed Jacob, after which you told us that fabricated story about how he did not wish to return to Herefordshire. I am going to make sure that you hang for this hideous crime.'

'No, no! You have got it all wrong.'

'I don't think so. You will hang, Rockstone.'

The thought of death swayed Rockstone more than prison. He paled, and after a moment, said, 'Alright, I will tell you the truth.'

'Go on.' Ravenscroft leaned back in his seat with some satisfaction.

'Jacob told me that he and this Lizzie Warren were lovers. One Sunday they met in the hills. They argued and she became angry. He pushed her away and she fell, hitting her head on a rock. Jacob saw that she was dead. He panicked and ran away. When the body was recovered, suspicion fell on him, so he left the country in a hurry, and went across to New York. That's what he told me. So, when we were with Walker's fair years later and he heard that the fair was going to Hereford, he said he did not wish to go there. He said there were powerful men who lived there, who if they recognised him would seek revenge for his part in the woman's death. That is all I know.'

'I see. Did Jacob say who these "powerful men" were?'

'No. That was all he said.'

'It is a pity he did not tell you who these men were.'

'Look, I am sorry I cannot help you further, Inspector, but what I am telling you is the truth. I never laid a hand on poor Jacob. I told him that it was all nonsense, that the people he alluded to were probably all dead or had long forgotten what had happened. He accepted what I said, but then of course we came to Hereford and that was the last I saw of him. I suppose I should have taken him more seriously at the time. I had no idea that someone was going to hang him from a tree.'

Ravenscroft looked intently at his suspect for a moment before turning towards Sergeant Morris. 'Take Mr Rockstone back to his cell.'

'I am telling you the truth, Ravenscroft. I did not kill Jacob. It was one of those men. You have to believe me,' protested Rockstone as Morris hauled his prisoner to his feet.

'I will speak with you later, Mr Rockstone,' said Ravenscroft, turning away.

'What will happen to me?' asked Rockstone as he was led towards the door.

'You will stand trial on multiple counts of breaking and entering, burglary, and deceiving the public.'

'So you believe me, about Jacob?' pleaded Rockstone.

Ravenscroft said nothing as Morris and Rockstone left the room.

'You do believe him, sir?' asked Crabb once the door had closed.

'I think he was telling us the truth, but I cannot be absolutely sure. Our American is a very clever and astute character, I have no doubt. He could have invented this story about these "powerful men" who were interested in taking revenge on poor Jacob, in an attempt to draw us away from what actually happened. If Rockstone's account is true then it is very annoying that Jacob did not tell him who these men were. Damn it, why is it at that our lives do not become any easier! Who were these "powerful men"? Rostagon? Sangster? Francis Constantine? Or was he referring to someone else we are yet to learn about?'

'There is someone else to consider,' said Crabb.

'Go on,' urged Ravenscroft.

'What about Thomas Temple? He shared a cell with Jacob while both men were in New York. We know that Jacob stole Temple's locket.'

'You think that Temple could have seen Jacob in Hereford, and recognised him, abducted and murdered him? It is a possibility of course, but would a man do all that because of a locket?'

'He was very attached to the keepsake. It contained the portrait of the mother he had never known; he had grown up with it, and it was his only link with the past.'

'Yes, but Jacob did not have the locket on him at the time of his death. If Temple wanted it back surely he would have compelled Jacob to lead him to where it was, if it meant that much to him. No, sorry, I just don't believe that Temple killed Jacob. Anyway we just don't know where Temple is now. We do know that he returned to England six years ago, but what happened to him after that remains a mystery.'

'Miss Constantine will be sad that we have not found her son.'

'We have done all that we can in that quarter. It is time we turned our attention towards Lizzie Warren. Tom, whereabouts is the original police file into her death?'

'It is back at the station in Ledbury. I managed to get it sent over from headquarters.'

'Then I think we should return there, but first I must instruct Sergeant Morris to proceed with the prosecutions of Rockstone and his accomplice.'

* * *

Ravenscroft sat in silence, reading the case notes into Lizzie Warren's death. Crabb busied himself tidying the books and papers on the shelves.

'It tells us nothing!' Ravenscroft sighed, as he flung the file on to the table. 'Accidental death caused by hitting her head on a rock as she fell. No other signs of violence. You say you have spoken with this former Inspector Robinson?'

'Yes, sir, and he confirmed what you have just said,' replied Crabb.

'Not a very detailed report. He interviewed both Rostagon and Sangster; that is all. There is no mention of Jacob. It is almost as though Robinson had made up his mind right from the beginning of the investigation, as to the cause of death. Perhaps I need to ask him some more questions.'

'What shall we do after that?'

'Go and see Rostagon and Sangster again, but—' Ravenscroft suddenly sat upright in his chair.

'Sir?' enquired Crabb.

'We may have been looking at this case from the wrong angle. I believe that when Mrs Ravenscroft read the newspaper report into Lizzie Warren's funeral, she discovered that the young woman had been buried without any relations being present.'

'That is so. We understand that both Lizzie's mother and the father were dead, and she had no brothers or sisters.'

'Where is Lizzie Warren buried?'

'In the graveyard at Little Malvern Priory Church.'

'I wonder why they chose to bury her there, of all places? I would have thought she would have been interned at Parkway where she worked, or at some other local church.'

'Perhaps her parents were also buried at Little Malvern?'

'You could be right. I think we should visit Little Malvern. Sometimes churchyards can reveal secrets about the living, as well as the dead.'

* * *

Ravenscroft opened the old wooden gate that led into the churchyard of Little Malvern Priory Church.

'See if you can find Lizzie Warren's grave. Someone may have put up a stone for her. I'll take this side,' suggested Ravenscroft.

The two detectives made their way amongst the rows of headstones, reading the inscriptions as they did so.

'Here we are, sir,' called Crabb after a few minutes had elapsed.

'What does the inscription say?' asked Ravenscroft, joining his companion.

'Not much. It just gives the name Lizzie Warren and the dates of her birth and death.'

'Is there nothing more?'

'No, the stone does not even include the mark of the stonemason who carved the inscription,' continued Crabb.

'That is unhelpful. Nevertheless, someone must have paid for this stone.'

'Francis Constantine? He was her godfather, after all, and we know he attended the funeral.'

'That is possible.'

'It is not much to show for a life, is it?'

Ravenscroft and Crabb quickly turned to see that the speaker was a young man dressed in clerical attire.

'Indeed not,' added Ravenscroft. 'I take it that you are the vicar here at Little Malvern?'

'Alas no, I am only the curate, Hugh Davis,' answered the clergyman. 'Can I be of any assistance to you gentlemen?'

'I hope so, Mr Davis. My name is Detective Inspector Ravenscroft and this is my associate, Constable Crabb. We have been investigating the death of the man found hanging on Hangman Hill.'

'Oh yes, I remember reading about it in the local newspaper. It was a terrible business. He is buried over there,' said the clergyman, pointing across the churchyard. 'Alas, there is no stone, only a simple wooden cross.'

'Indeed, but what concerns us at the moment is the young woman here, Lizzie Warren. She also died on the hill some ten years ago.'

'I have heard of the event, but of course I was not at Malvern then. I have only been curate here for the past year or so.'

'I thought I had not seen you before,' said Crabb.

'This is only my second position since I joined the church five years ago.'

'Oh, where were you before you came here Mr Davis?' asked Ravenscroft.

'After being ordained, I was a curate in Dudley.'

'You must find this quite a change?' suggested Ravenscroft.

'Indeed. It is so much more peaceful here. I would not wish to be anywhere else,' said the clergyman giving a broad smile.

'I wonder if we might trouble you to look at the church records?' asked Ravenscroft, returning to the matter in hand.

'Certainly,' replied the young man. 'If you would care to follow me inside, gentlemen, I will be glad to show them to you.'

Ravenscroft and Crabb followed the clergyman into the interior of the church.

'The parish registers are kept in this oak chest here,' said the curate, pointing to the piece of furniture in the corner. 'I'll bring them over to you at the table.'

Ravenscroft and Crabb waited as the chest was unlocked and the old volumes brought over to them.

'Perhaps we could start with the burial entry for Lizzie Warren,' suggested Ravenscroft.

The clergyman opened one of the volumes and turned over the pages.

'Yes, there we are. Name, occupation, address, and date of burial,' said Ravenscroft, examining the entry. 'There is nothing unusual there. I believe that Lizzie Warren may also have been baptised here. Might we look at the records for twenty-one years before this date?'

The curate reached for another volume and again turned the pages. 'Ah, I think this may be what you are looking for, Inspector.'

'"Lizzie Warren, baptised 10 September, daughter of Stephen Warren and his wife Mary,"' said Ravenscroft, reading the entry aloud. 'We believe that Lizzie had no brothers or sisters?'

'We can go through the pages covering the years before and after that date,' suggested the curate.

Ravenscroft searched through the register. 'No, there are no further entries, so there would appear to be no siblings. I wonder if Lizzie's parents were also married here in this church. Lizzie was born in early 1860, so we would need to look for the years preceding that date.'

The clergyman placed a larger volume on the table, and turned over the pages.

'Yes, here we are. Marriage of Stephen Warren and Mary — Goodness me!' exclaimed Ravenscroft, pointing at the entry. 'See here, Tom, do you see Mary Warren's maiden name!'

'Yes, sir. That puts a new complexion on the case.'

'It does indeed. Let us return to Lizzie Warren's grave. I would not be surprised if we discover some graves nearby of people with the same family name as this. Thank you, Mr Davis, you have been most helpful.'

Ravenscroft and Crabb quickly made their way out of the small church and returned to Lizzie Warren's grave.

'It is just as I thought!' exclaimed Ravenscroft. 'See the name on this stone next to Lizzie's.'

'It's the same family name on this one as well, sir,' said Crabb.

'We should have come here earlier. Lizzie was buried amongst her ancestors. How stupid we have been. I see it all now. Now we know not only who killed Jacob, but also why. It is time we paid a visit to our murderer.'

CHAPTER FIFTEEN

HEREFORDSHIRE

Inspector Ravenscroft alighted from the trap outside the small cottage at Eastnor and walked up the garden path, closely followed by Crabb.

As they neared the door it was opened by an elderly grey-haired man.

'Caleb Robinson?' said Ravenscroft.

'Huh, I thought ye would be back.'

'May we come in?'

'If ye must.'

'I have to tell you that we know all about Lizzie Warren. Her mother was Mary Robinson, your sister, I believe. Lizzie Warren was your niece.'

'It took you a long time to work that out,' muttered Caleb.

'It was you who saw poor Jacob at the fair in Hereford, and who returned the following night with your accomplice. Together, you captured Jacob, brought him out here to Hangman Hill and strung him up there on one of the trees. Then, when you were sure he was dead, you walked down to the inn to report that you had found the body on your walk in the hills. It was also very clever of you, telling us that fanciful story of the horseman in the wood, in the hope that it would throw us off the scent. Your big mistake was not searching the lining of Jacob's coat. Everything we have learned about this case came from one small box of pills he had on him,' said Ravenscroft.

'Jacob got what was coming to him. He killed our beautiful Lizzie that morning on the hill. She didn't deserve to die. She were an innocent young lass until she met that awful man. He violated her and then he killed her. He escaped justice by running off to America, but I knew it was him when I saw him at that fair in Hereford that night. He deserved everything that was coming to him. I ain't sorry for what we did.'

'Lizzie Warren died as the result of an accident,' said Crabb.

'Accident? How do you know that? No, he killed her, and that's no mistake.'

'You cannot take the law into your own hands,' said Ravenscroft.

'The law!' growled Robinson. 'The law did not help to bring justice for our Lizzie.'

'Crabb, put the cuffs on him.'

'I knew you would be back. I don't cares what will happen to me now. I'm an old man. Jacob paid for what he did to our Lizzie.'

'You will hang, just as poor Jacob did,' said Ravenscroft. 'Perhaps the hangman will show a greater consideration towards you than you displayed towards Jacob. I also know who your accomplice was. We have him in custody now. He has told us everything.'

Robinson laughed. 'So you got Alfred as well. He won't tell you anything.'

Ravenscroft looked at Crabb. 'Alfred Robinson, the former police inspector at Malvern, who carried out the investigation into Lizzie Warren's death. He is your brother, I believe. I wonder, was it you or Alfred who placed the rope around Jacob's neck?'

'That's for you to find out,' retorted Robinson.

'It was your brother who discovered that Lizzie had arranged to meet Jacob that morning on Hangman Hill, but he made no mention in his report that Jacob might have been responsible for her death. That was because he knew that the police authorities had no evidence against him, but before you and Alfred could take the law into your own hands, Jacob left the county in a hurry and went to America.'

'You knows it all. Clever, ain't you,' muttered the hand-cuffed man.

'Your brother was arrested two hours ago. He denied all knowledge of the murder of Jacob. However you have just now confirmed his guilt. Both of you will stand trial for the murder of Jacob. Take him to the trap, Tom.'

* * *

'They will both hang, of course,' said Ravenscroft, as he and Lucy sat at the breakfast table the following morning.

'What a terrible thing to have done,' remarked Lucy. 'That poor man Jacob.'

'Yes, and if it had not been for you, my dear, justice would never have been done. It was clever of you to go to the Reading Rooms in Malvern and look through past issues of the local newspaper to see if there had been any previous crimes committed on Hangman Hill. It was the account of Lizzie Warren's death that provided us with the information we needed to solve this case. Tom and I had given all our attention to finding that scoundrel Rockstone. You should have been a detective.'

'Are there any female detectives in the police force?' asked Lucy.

'I do not know of any. Perhaps I should put your name forward,' laughed Ravenscroft.

'I have more than enough to occupy my time here, looking after two children and running this house.'

'And a very good job you make of it, as well. I suppose the ironic thing about this case, was that one of the murderers was standing right by my side at the start of our enquiries, when we found Jacob on Hangman Hill. It was only when I finally read Alfred Robinson's report into the death of Lizzie Warren that my suspicions were aroused. There was hardly any detail in the policeman's report, and he seemed anxious to end his investigation as soon as possible. I just knew then that the answer might just lie in the churchyard in Little Malvern where Lizzie was buried. When we returned to look at her grave, we could see that there were other stones nearby belonging to members of the Robinson family.'

'Well, I am pleased that the case has come to a satisfactory conclusion.'

'But it has not for Maria Constantine. We have still not found her son, despite my travelling halfway round the world.'

'You tried your hardest Samuel. It must be some consolation to her that you were able to tell her about how her son was looked after by the Foundling Hospital, and how he secured that position at Mincing and Stricket in London, and then went to America,' said Lucy.

'Where he ended up in prison,' interjected Ravenscroft.

'Only for a short while, before he was taken on at Macy's. They must have thought highly of him. I wonder why he decided to leave New York. Macy's does sound rather splendid, from the description you gave of it, and I do so like that silk shawl that you brought back for me. It was so kind of you.'

'I'm pleased you like it,' smiled Ravenscroft. He picked up his newspaper and resumed his reading.

'Samuel, I don't suppose you still have that locket?' said Lucy, looking up again from her sewing.

'As a matter of fact, I do,' replied Ravenscroft reaching into his pocket. 'I have taken this locket halfway round the world with me. Now I suppose I must return it to Miss Constantine.'

'May I have another look at it? I have not seen it since that night when you acquired it from Rockstone, and I should just like one further look at it before you give it back.'

'Here you are, my dear.' Ravenscroft passed the item to his wife.

'It is such a beautiful portrait, and so well executed. I can see the resemblance quite clearly. Although it was painted by that Frenchman some thirty years ago, you would still know that it was Maria Constantine if you saw her today. The nose, and mouth, and that look in the eyes,' said Lucy studying the miniature.

'Yes, I recognised the sitter as soon as I saw her.'

'Excuse me, sir, the morning post has just arrived,' said the maid, entering the room.

'Thank you, Susan.'

'A letter from America. Must be from Richardson, the Pinkerton agent I told you about,' said Ravenscroft examining the envelope. 'I must write to him and tell him what happened to O'Callaghan.'

'How exciting,' said Lucy.

Ravenscroft opened the letter and read aloud its contents —

Ravenscroft,

Thought you might be interested in receiving the enclosed photograph.

After your departure yesterday, I paid a visit to Macy's — my brother-in-law is the senior clerk there. He made another search through the archives, and we found this photograph. It shows the staff members of the China Department posing for the camera. I asked around and one or two of the people remembered your Thomas Temple. Apparently he is the second man in the back row.

I hope this is of some assistance to you.

Good luck,
Bill Richardson.

'That is most fortunate,' said Lucy.

'Where is the magnifying glass?' asked Ravenscroft, studying the enclosed photograph.

'I believe it is on the sideboard over there.'

Ravenscroft rose from the table, picked up the lens and took the photograph over to the window. 'Good Lord!'

'Whatever is it, Samuel?' asked a startled Lucy.

'I can see it now! This man in the photograph, I can see the resemblance now — the same eyes, nose and mouth. Good heavens! I would never have guessed it. Thomas Temple has been here all the time!'

EPILOGUE

As he took the locket from Ravenscroft's outstretched hand, tears began to form in the man's eyes.

'You must forgive me, Inspector Ravenscroft, but I never expected to see this again. How did you come by it?'

'The dead man, Jacob Kelly, had it concealed amongst his private effects,' replied Ravenscroft.

'I am sorry, but you say Jacob is dead?'

'He was the dead man found hanging from a tree on Hangman Hill several weeks ago.'

'Yes, I recall reading about the incident in the local paper, but the report did not name the victim.'

'At that time we had not been able to identify the body. I am pleased to say that his killers have now been apprehended.'

'But why would anyone want to kill poor Jacob?'

'It is rather a long story, but it seems that he may have been involved in Lizzie Warren's death on Hangman Hill, ten years ago before he went to America. His killers evidently concluded that Jacob had murdered Lizzie, and when they saw that he had returned to Hereford they took the law into their own hands.'

'This lady in the locket, I always knew that she was my mother. I say that because when I was growing up at the

Foundling Hospital in London I always believed that I had been given away by someone who must have once cared a great deal for me, and as I was growing up I imagined this beautiful woman who one day would come back and claim me. Then when I left the Hospital at the age of fifteen they gave me the locket, saying that its owner had been a gentlewoman from Herefordshire. That was all they would say, and as I lay in my bed at night during the coming years, I would take out the locket, and open it, and place it on the pillow by the side of my head, and look at those features and knew that she had once loved me, and that something terrible must have happened shortly after my birth that compelled her to give me up.'

'She was a single woman. The scandal would have destroyed both her and her family,' said Ravenscroft quietly.

'I was employed as a junior clerk at Mincing and Stricket in London for four years, and then one day they learned that their agent in New York had been killed in some public house brawl, and they asked if I would like to take on the position,' continued the other. 'As I was keen to see the world at this time, I readily accepted, but the position was not as I had imagined it. Their warehouse was situated in a not very attractive area of the city, and I was compelled to live out a lonely existence at Ma Scrivens' Lodging House in Manhattan. Then one day the police authorities raided the building where I worked and they found some stolen items amongst our goods, and I was arrested. I was entirely innocent of this crime, you must believe me, Inspector Ravenscroft, but although I pleaded my case I was found guilty and sentenced to three years' imprisonment on Blackwell's Island. Often in my cell I would take out that locket and look at that face, and I promised myself that one day, when I was free, I would return to England and find my mother.'

'I understand that you shared a cell with Jacob? Did he ever tell you about why he had been forced to leave England?' asked Ravenscroft.

'No, he told me nothing of his past life. Jacob was in my cell for only a few weeks, then he was released, and once he had gone I made the terrible discovery that he had somehow appropriated the locket. Imagine my anguish, Inspector. The one possession that I valued above even my own life had been taken from me! I was distraught, but I still had the memories, and when I closed my eyes I could still see her face, and that gave me the strength to go on.'

'How did you gain employment at Macy's?'

'Because I had received a good education at the Foundling Hospital, I was able to put that to use in helping a number of the inmates to read and write. The Warden learned of my industry, thought that I should be given a fresh start in life, and said that he would do all that he could to see that I would secure honest employment upon my release. One of his friends was a partner in Macy's, and that was how I went to work at the department store. It was like a palace to me, and after all the drab unhappy years of loneliness, it seemed almost like home working there. For a while I was happy there, but all the time I was there I thought of nothing but England, and of my mother.

'Eventually I saved enough money for the return passage to Liverpool. I did not know where my mother lived, but the Foundling Hospital said she had come from Herefordshire, and so I came to this part of the country, where I was fortunate to gain employment. I thought it expedient to change my name. I wanted to put the past behind me. It was to be a new beginning. My work has bought me a great deal of satisfaction over the years, Inspector Ravenscroft, but I have always lived in the hope that one day I would see my mother again and that we would be united.'

'I have to tell you that your mother has never forgotten you, and like you has thought constantly that one day you will be together,' said Ravenscroft, once the man had finished his account.

'And this is the house where she lives?' he asked as the trap pulled up on the road outside the Verzons. 'It is a fine building.'

'Miss Constantine lives here with her brother,' said Crabb, bringing the horse to a standstill.

The man stepped down from the trap. 'I cannot thank you enough. Will you come with me? I am sure that my mother would wish to express her gratitude to you in person.'

'I have taken the liberty of sending your mother a telegram this morning. She is expecting you. I think we will not intrude at this time. I wish you well,' smiled Ravenscroft.

'Thank you once again, Inspector.'

Ravenscroft and Crabb watched as Ronald Clifford, the Malvern librarian, opened the gates to the Verzons, and with one last wave disappeared from view.

'So, a satisfactory end to the case, would you not say so, Tom?' said Ravenscroft.

'Most satisfactory.' Crabb urged the horse forward.

'To think that I went halfway round the world looking for Maria Constantine's son, and all the time he was living not eight miles from Ledbury.'

'It is a strange world, sir.'

'Oh, I nearly forgot, this letter arrived for you this morning. Give me the reins while you look at it.' Ravenscroft removed an envelope from his inside coat pocket and passed it over, with a broad smile, to his constable. 'I had a word with the Superintendent before I left for America.'

'A letter for me. It looks very formal,' said Crabb hesitantly.

'I think you will be pleased when you read its contents.'

Crabb tore open the envelope and read the lines, before exclaiming, 'My word! I don't believe it, sir. I don't deserve this.'

'You most certainly do. Congratulations, Detective Sergeant Crabb, upon a richly deserved promotion!'

THE END

Please join our mailing list for free Kindle historical fiction, sagas, romance books, mysteries and crime thrillers, and new releases!

www.joffebooks.com

FREE KINDLE BOOKS

Made in United States
North Haven, CT
23 August 2022

23143814R00125